HYDROGEN RUNNER

HYDROGEN RUNNER

CLAUDIA K LEBER

DEDICATIONS

I wish to thank my entire family for all their suggestions. Special thanks to Amanda who's help, and attention to content was invaluable. I wish to dedicate Hydrogen Runner to man's - evolving future. Ever as we stand on each other's shoulders and discoveries.

ABOUT THE AUTHOR

Claudia K. Leber was born in the American Hospital in Paris, France to a US Army soldier and a French nursing assistant. She traveled extensively during her life as her father taught in various universities. She attended high school in Perth Australia, and upon return to the U.S. started college at the University of California in Irvine where she received a BA in Chemistry and worked at the Chemistry department nuclear research reactor. Then while attending the University of California at Riverside she studied Geology and met her future husband while receiving a secondary teaching credential. Her studies continued at the dental school of Washington University in St. Louis where she received her DMD degree. It's because of her love of Chemistry and Science that 'Hydrogen Runner' materialized. Now retired, she fills her life with family and grandchildren.

CHAPTER 1

PREPARE TO RUN

"Damn, four years since my last hydrogen run." Martin Mercer thought to himself, amazed that the time had passed so quickly. Although regular trips to the sun every four years were enough to ensure financial security for his family, that wasn't what kept Martin making runs, when most 42-year-old pilots had long-since left running to the younger eager beavers. "No, it's not the money," he thought, stretching his legs out under his desk and running his fingers through his hair. Hydrogen running could never be considered easy money. To Martin, it was the anticipation of unexpected danger, the adventure of previously unexplored space, and if the truth be told, the absolute freedom of being a runner was what he found most appealing.

Hydrogen has become one of the world's most valuable resources. Global adoption of fusion power plants became a reality in 2125. Advancements in nuclear fusion have been at the forefront of energy research for the past millennium. The universe taught us that hydrogen is a remarkable energy source. The prime example being that the very stars that light up our skies are giant nuclear reactors. Mankind understood that it could be done, but mastering fusion was like the perpetual carrot-on-a-stick. The first fusion power plant was the result of a multinational effort. The participating nations helped spread the burden of funding and, in turn, allowed each group to identify specific variables that would overcome the hurdles necessary to achieve the massive temperatures, pressure and confinement for hydrogen atoms to fuse into helium.

Even before the advent of fusion, the use of hydrogen as a fuel source had always been stunted by the generation of pure hydrogen from current resources here on earth. The general problem with hydrogen production is the energy costs necessary to produce it. The most economical method of obtaining hydrogen is from the breakdown of organics, such as natural gas. However, the environmental issues inherent in working with hydrocarbon fuels remain; during the process of reforming hydrocarbons into hydrogen, carbon monoxide is released. The ideal source of hydrogen is in fact water through electrolysis. Electrolysis, however, is incredibly energy intensive; the use of electricity to break down water into hydrogen and oxygen is a much more environmentally friendly practice, but less of an economical one.

This sent mankind searching for more readily available sources of hydrogen. Hydrogen may make up less than 0.003% of the earth's atmosphere, but the universe is loaded with the stuff. The only problem is being how to get it, and how to safely bring the fuel back to Earth. Hydrogen is after all extremely combustible when exposed to air and transporting it through Earth's atmosphere can become dicey. If you are willing to man regular trips to space, you likely aren't going to bat an eye at what you're bringing back. It's just one more hazard that hydrogen runners had to handle correctly to avoid an explosive finale.

Martin put his pen down and leaned forward to rub his tired eyes. "These goddamn forms have tripled since last time," he thought as he stared at the mountains of paperwork that would need to be completed before his next run in mid-February. He pulled one form from the bottom of the stack, a runner's life insurance policy. He scanned the rates and groaned as he flipped the page over. His age bracket had fallen to the second page. Somehow runner's life insurance always felt like he was betting on the world that he wasn't coming back, except it's a bet he loved losing. It didn't mean he liked placing the bet in the first place, though. His eyes landed on the picture on his desk of Al, Nicole, and himself, taken at a Texan's game ten years ago. Al had been his classmate and occasional co-pilot during runs. He locked eyes with Al in the picture, picked up his pen again and finished filling out the insurance forms before putting them back at the bottom of the pile to hide them from Nicole.

Losing Al had been a big hit. The one real time Martin considered a new career; one that would keep him Earth-bound. Martin would never find another runner who understood his penchant for skipping the details and jumping headfirst into the challenge. He wasn't careless, but he had damn good instincts, only something that 20 years of running could give you. Hearing the whispers behind his back after the accident was hard though. People were saying that perhaps more attention could have been given to the temperature control unit where the hydrogen collectors were stored during the flight. Or, that the safety alarm systems on board were not properly tested before take-off. He had tried to ignore the idiots, but every once in a while, the sidelong glances and condescending attitudes got to him. "Oh, get over it, Martin!" He told himself, knowing things tended to hit him heavier just before a run.

"Honey, what are you working on?" His wife interrupted, breaking the funk Martin was about to fall into.

"Oh... well uh... Nicole, it's time for another run, honey!" Martin said, avoiding eye contact with his wife, wanting to postpone her disapproval as long as possible. When he looked up, he couldn't help but grin. The sight of her with her hands on her hips and that when-were-we-going-to-discuss-this look spreading across her face and body language like a tidal wave. It didn't take much, even after 19 years of marriage, to make him want to sweep this feisty woman up in his arms. That was the hard part about running. Every day sleeping alone, seeing nothing but unshaven male faces and the occasional cold and wispy hologram of a telecommute.

For years, Nicole had been after him to take that job at the Agency with her brother, John. "You're planning another run," she said. It wasn't a question. "Don't you want to rethink this, Marty? With your experience, you don't have to be a runner!"

Martin had good instincts, but that didn't always mean he had common sense, "Well baby, you could always try to convince me." He teased.

She bubbled over; her quick glance around the room telling him that she was likely looking for the nearest and most convenient thing to throw at him. "Martin if you keep grinning at me like that, I swear...!" She stomped.

He jumped up and crossed the room to her, "I'm sorry baby. I was going to talk to you about it at dinner tonight. Maybe I shouldn't go this time...but the Agency? Sitting behind a tidy desk, spending one uneventful day after another scheduling runners. You know I'd go crazy working for someone else. Let alone cooped up in an office all day, trapped by the problems your brother must contend with. If you ask me, John's got too many chiefs and not enough Indians at that agency of his. I don't want to be a part of the power struggle, Nicole. It's nuts over there. Com'on - you've heard your brother talk about that place - everybody telling him what to do and when he can do it! Do you really think I could stand that shit?"

Martin knew he had to be where the action was, where he knew it was up to him to make the difference. "I don't want a boss hanging over my shoulder every minute!"

"I worry, that's all Martin! Every time we have this conversation, I get nowhere! I don't want to talk about it anymore!" She said, her eyes turning a little red as she held back tears.

"Now, don't get that look, Nicole. I've been running for over 20 years, and I've never come up against a problem I couldn't figure out or avoid, have I?"

She looked away from him; he knew her eyes were staring at the back of the picture of Al on his desk. "When are you planning on going? Will you be able to plan your run around Wendy's birthday, at least, Martin?" She turned to look at him again, real tears threatening to fall, "I hate to think of you being out there all by yourself."

"Aww baby," he said taking her in his arms, "I'll tell you what I'm going to do." Regardless of Martin's joking demeanor, he had anticipated his wife's mood. "Yes, I will be here for Wendy's birthday, and I won't be out there all by myself. I'm going to give George a call and see if he wants to initiate one of the new cadets on a novice run with me. Would that set your mind to rest?" He asked, hoping his old instructor would be able to persuade Nicole of the importance of training these pups with a seasoned veteran like himself.

"I just wish you weren't gone for so long Marty."

Unfortunately, both Martin and Nicole knew that the best places to fill a hydrogen collector is very near the sun when flares shoot hydrogen out into the surrounding area or from a gas giant such as Jupiter. A run to the sun usually took about 200 days, providing the flares cooperate, which isn't always the case. A run to Jupiter could take three to four years. Martin had always been a sun runner. People could argue until they were blue in the face that Jupiter runs were safer, but Martin would call "bullshit" every single time. Sun runners are in space less than a year. That, in Martin's book, is safer. There was more risk that the mission could fail, but Martin's collectors had always made it back.

His longest run lasted 267 days He had particularly bad luck in retrieving his collectors. Timing is very critical in making a good catch. If the collector is sent out too early, it may be eaten by the heat from the actual flare. If one waits too long the hydrogen has already dissipated into space making the collection less profitable. Naturally one must send out a collector because the heat is too great for ships to get too close to the sun. Then, there is the minor problem of the returning collector being pirated on its way back. Space pirate... Nicole should count her lucky stars. There is worse careers Martin could have chosen.

Martin knew he was not going to be able to comfort Nicole. Leaving his family during the run was part of the job description, a part he did not like either. He knew the best thing he could do now was to change the subject. "Do you believe we're already into the year 2135?" Talking about the kids would do the trick. "Wendy's going to be 16-Lance is, going to be...huh..."

"Fourteen, dear." Nicole scolded.

"Yea, and life is good!" He continued, in a hurry to cover up his slip about Lance's age. Lance was such a quirky kid. He was either under his father's skin all the time, or doing something that was forgettable. Martin loved Lance, but for the hundredth time, he wondered why he couldn't have had a son who loved to play laser tag outside with his friends instead of virtual reality, role-playing games in his room. It confused Martin how Lance seemed to want to be an observer of life instead of a participant, but he knew better than to go there with Nicole. "We've made a good life for ourselves, haven't we, baby? Is that a smile?"

She wasn't smiling, but his enthusiasm seemed to dam up the flow of tears enough for her to regain her composure. Nicole had always hated crying. She pulled away from him and turned to leave his office, "We're not done talking about this Marty." She said as she walked down the hall.

Martin got a bit miffed with her as he watched her turn the corner to the kitchen.

"She always has to have the last word, even when I'm telecommuting from a mission 80,000,000 miles from home." He thought to himself, as he turned back to his paperwork.

"Know what? I don't feel like cooking tonight. Let's see if George and Rita want to go out for a bite." She called back over her shoulder as she stepped into the hallway.

"Okay, let me finish up here and make some calls to get an assigned ship and a scheduled launch." The government was more than cooperative with independent runners, provided they would be considered first when it came time to sell the hydrogen. However, if you put the fuel up for bid with another government upon your return, good luck trying to schedule another run sponsored by the agency. Just last year, a friend of Martin's had received a dynamite offer from Germany for his load, and he couldn't resist the temptation to make twice what the United States had offered. He'd been regretting his sellout ever since.

"Oh, hello!" He replied to the person on the other end of the phone. "Martin Mercer, here. I'd like to schedule a hydrogen run for February 15th, please. Yes, my licenses are current," he continued, slightly irritated with the tiresome questions of some flunky at the very Agency where Nicole wanted him to work. "Yes, within two days of that date will be fine. Thank you. I'll be waiting to hear back from you."

"So, what about dinner, Marty?" Nicole questioned, as she peeked her head into the office.

"Yeah, I'm done for the day. Do you want me to give George and Rita a call since I need to talk to him about the cadet?" He asked, trying to appease her after their little spat.

"Yeah, you call while I get ready," which meant Martin would have a good thirty minutes to chat with George.

"Hey, George? How's retired life treating you?" Martin asked. It was always good to talk with his old teacher. They had been through quite a few adventures together when hydrogen running was a lot less sophisticated.

"Why, you old scalawag! It sure is good to hear from you, Marty," George replied, happy to hear a familiar voice.

"So, what about you and Rita coming out to dinner with Nicole and me? I need you to do some heavy talkin', my friend."

"What have you done now? This could be the most excitement I've had all week. I'm tellin' you, I'm not quite ready for the porch and rocker yet," answered George. "Working as a consultant with these young cadets can turn you old before your time, though. I swear, during each maiden run I've thought it was all over more times than I care to mention!"

"And you want me to take one of these kids on a run with me?" joked Martin.

"Don't worry, nobody but the best for you, Marty! I wondered when you were going to be making your next run!" George stated. "Oh, now I get what the dinner invite is all about. Is Nicole giving you grief about running again?"

"Yep! The only thing that somewhat pacified her was a promise that I'd take one of your young pups along."

"She knows you won't take chances with somebody else's life, that's why!" George commented. "She should know by now I wouldn't let anything happen to you. It would ruin my rep; know what I mean?" George laughed. "I'll let my cadet know you said yes.

He'll be thrilled. I have Joe Burwick in mind. He's top in his class and perfect for you."

"How do you mean?" Martin questioned.

"This whiz kid is a real stickler for details. I can't wait. He'll drive you crazy! I'll tell Nicole you'll be home in half the time with Joe along! When do Rita and I meet you for dinner?" George choked out, still laughing as he thought of the two of them together for seven or eight months on this run.

"How about the usual place at-say 7:00?"

"Sure, see you soon," replied George.

Martin hung up the phone and immediately began regretting his promise to Nicole to take somebody along on this trip. "What have I gotten myself into?" He spoke the question out loud. "I would rather have my own space," he thought, chuckling to himself at the unintended pun as he rose from his desk. Just a few more things to fill out before tomorrow's trip to the Space Center. Nicole had already arranged an 11:00 a.m. luncheon with her brother John. Martin figured he would make use of the trip since there was no way he was going to be recruited to a desk job.

* * * * *

The entrance to the Space Center was quite impressive, with its high technology, x-ray throughways and military-like attendants monitoring the checkpoints. There were two gates at each sector: one that relied solely on electronics, computers and ultrasonic equipment, the other manned by an expert security officer. After passing through the first gate, the security official had the task of overseeing the retinal scan and allocating a visitor's pass that would allow or limit access to necessary areas within the facility. Any suspicious person could be detained for hours until Agency headquarters were satisfied that all was on the up and up. To think people thought airline security was a hassle.

Martin placed his access card into the electronic slot of the first gate, then walked through the ultrasonic detector to match his internal structure to that contained in his computer file as he waved nonchalantly to the security official. Next, he was detained between the two gates while a computer voice requested that he approach the retinal scanner. As soon as clearance was given, Marty was given his visitor access pass and escorted to an electric car, provided by the Agency for their VIPs. "I'm really getting the executive treatment today," he thought, wondering what they wanted from him in return. "Hi Rob. Staying out of trouble?" Asked Martin of the vehicle attendant.

"Just barely." Rob answered.

"Good job! I remember when I was living on the edge. What a life, hey?" Martin asked, convinced this kid didn't have a clue as to what real trouble was.

"Off on another run?" Rob questioned.

"Yeah, it's that time again." Marty responded.

"Well, best of luck to you then," replied Rob while getting ready for the next visitor to come through the gates.

Martin headed straight for the administration building to make sure his shuttle reservations were in order. He quickly checked his optical computer, glad to see there was still time before the luncheon date with his brother-in-law, John. As he approached the administration building, he marveled at how mammoth the complex was, and how many people it took to coordinate all the activities within its walls. "How did people find their way around in this maze?" He thought to himself. Yet, this complex was a daily, eight-hour reality to many of the people working at the Agency.

As he stepped up to the transport, a digital voice asked, "What is your destination, please?"

"Shuttle scheduling office." Marty replied as he passed his visitor pass under the transporter's scanner. "Level one or two, Mr. Mercer?" The computer voice asked, addressing him by name after properly identifying him.

"Level one!" Within a matter of seconds, Martin arrived at his requested destination. The moment the beam cleared, he found his contact.

"Helen, Helen, Helen, how are you, sweetheart?" asked Martin, grinning from ear to ear while approaching the serious-faced, older woman sitting behind the metal counter. She had been with the Agency for years, and Martin knew her skills must make her indispensable, otherwise why would they keep such a sourpuss around for so long. It had gotten to be a joke with all the pilots to see if any of them could make her crack a smile. Just once even a chuckle would do! So far, none had succeeded.

"I'm fine, thank you, Mr. Mercer," Helen said in the same monotone voice she used on everybody, VIPs as well as runners.

"Helen, I thought you'd be retired by now!" Martin commented.

"And I you, sir." she said, matching his wit for wit without cracking a smile.

"Touché ole' girl! How's the scheduling going for my run?" He inquired.

"You are ready to go," she answered in her efficient manner.

"Oh, I almost forgot to let you know, Helen. I'll be taking along one of George's cadets. Hope that doesn't throw wrench into things!" He said, preparing himself for her disapproval.

He wasn't to be disappointed when Helen gave him a sharp look, saying, "It does, but I'm sure that will not matter one iota to your plans, now will it Mr. Mercer? Give me his name, please, and I will do the rest." She continued with a growing scowl quickly spreading down her face like a shade being lowered on the world.

"I love you, Helen! If you and I weren't married, I'd snap you up in a minute!" He joked. "The cadet's name is Joe Burwick, and George can give you the run-down on him."

"Fine, I will keep you informed as to the progress of your scheduled run." Helen said, dismissing him with her sternness.

"Yea, well, I'll be going now. Got a luncheon date with John Mc Douglas. Take care, sweetheart!" He commented receiving zero reaction from Helen as usual. He hurried toward the double doors and down the hall in what he believed to be the direction of the cafeteria. Martin began navigating his way through the endless corridors and levels, wondering if he would ever find the eatery. Finally, he spotted John sitting outside on the patio, and with a wave, his brother-in-law motioned him over.

"Guess you know it's time for our four-year talk," John commented, as he stood to give Martin a hug.

"It's a matter of money, John. Nicole likes the good life, but in order to give that to her, I've got to run!" He said almost defensively.

"Marty, you forget who you're talking to. It's John here. Remember me, I'm the one who knows the real story behind all this self-sacrificing talk about running. I've been around too many runners in my time to fall for that line of horse shit!" John said as he cleared the chair of files so that Martin could sit down.

"It's a dirty job, John, but somebody has to do it!" Martin laughed, entertained by John's sincerity when it came to these little talks.

"Yea, but Nicole wants that somebody to be a person other than her husband. You know, Martin, there are those of us who make a pretty good living without running. Don't you think it's about time to let some of these younger cadets take over?" John continued trying to discourage Martin from taking this run. He didn't have a good feeling about this trip, but he didn't want to lay that one on his brother-in-law.

"Actually, I will be taking along a young cadet of George's. Now you and Nicole can relax, right?" He asked, knowing that John hated this little tit for tat conversation even more than he did.

"Seriously Martin, there is a way to earn some extra money without running, and you'll be happy to hear it isn't working for the Agency either." Put in John, confident Martin wouldn't entertain any position with the government.

"So, let's hear it. I'm all ears," said Martin in a somewhat bored tone.

"The science department is willing to pay for the safe transport of supplies to the SOHOI station. They are in a bit of a bind, since losing their contract through UniExpress. Did you know they have eliminated SOHOIII from their regular delivery route? They claim it just wasn't profitable for them to continue that route any longer, so to make a long story short, we want you to carry some extra cargo for us. What do you say?" John asked, expecting Martin's answer to be what he wanted to hear. After all, the Agency pays well for delivery jobs, and he knew Martin could often be motivated by money.

"Might as well. I'll be stopping there anyway." Martin responded. He liked visiting the Solar and Heliospheric Observatory III (SOHOIII), seeing first-hand the progress of his favorite biosystem, Gila, and his (Is it supposed to be 'his or 'its'?) newest developments.

"Great! My superiors will be very appreciative!" John said. Ready to move on to a conversation about the Agency. His topics didn't change much from meeting to meeting, or person to person. He was always ready to complain to willing listeners about the Agency. It had become the trendy thing to do, and John wasn't averse to passing on stories of its' political battles, proudly announcing how his skillful art of diplomacy had kept him from having to stick his neck out too far.

"I've always stuck my neck out as far as it would go, I think," Martin commented. "Whether it be to help a friend or to stand up for what I believe, I'm afraid I couldn't play your game, John. I've been screwed before by people who mean well, but don't have the balls to stand up for someone, or by those who are so afraid of something or someone that they won't speak their mind. I guess diplomacy has never been my strong suit."

"If you came aboard, Marty, I could be a buffer for you. I know the Agency well enough that I could find a place where you would be least affected by petty problems!" John continued, anxious to press his point for Nicole's sake.

"I didn't know a place like that existed in the Agency," Martin said as he chuckled beneath his breath. "Let's see how this run goes. If George's student works out, maybe I'll continue running for a while longer 'til my legs go on me. Otherwise, I might take you up on your offer. I appreciate your concern, John, but I'm just not cut out for an office job, you know? I seem to have a problem with administrative type people, or bosses in general, for that matter. Besides, some of them have memories that last a lifetime, and I'm afraid I don't have a reputation for reading the fine print."

"If you're talking about Al, Marty, nobody holds you responsible for that accident. God, you need to let go of that. It was a long time ago, and most around here don't even remember it. They have trouble remembering what happened yesterday with themselves, much less ten years ago with somebody else!" John said, sensitive to Martin's pain when it came to the death of his friend.

As the two finished their comfortable meal eaten on the currently being staffed climate-controlled patio, they ended their luncheon talking about the new Jupiter station that was with great minds and designed with unbelievable technology. Parting company, Martin found himself somewhat comforted John's offer of a job at the Agency, even though he could never imagine himself accepting. All he wanted to think about now was running-the launch-blast off!

CHAPTER 2

DEPARTURE

"Well, you'll be leaving tomorrow." Said Nicole, stirring Marty awake as she turned toward him with her sleepless eyes.

"Yea," mumbled Marty, half-asleep and dog tired from all the activities of the last few days. "So, how do you think Wendy enjoyed her birthday party?" The virtual getaway had been expensive for them to treat Wendy and her friends to, but Martin was feeling especially generous just before his run, and he suspected Wendy took advantage of that fact. Like her father, she has good instincts!

"Oh, I don't know. Virtual surfing on a beach in Sydney. I'm pretty sure she hated it," she said as she teased him. "The private concert in the beach house though was pretty impressive. She's in love with that band. How did they get the holograms to be so interactive? I thought Wendy was going to pass out when the lead vocalist did that acoustic serenade for her. You've outdone yourself this time, Martin, and there's going to be hell to pay trying to top this year's celebration next year," Nicole scolded, confident that Wendy would cook up something equally as entertaining and expensive.

"Well, sweet sixteen is supposed to be memorable, don't you think?" Martin defended, feeling that the fun everybody had was well worth the heavy hit to his pocketbook.

"It meant a lot to her that you were there, especially knowing how much work you had going in preparation for this run." Nicole reached over and pulled Martin close as she continued saying, "I really do appreciate your participation, Marty. Let's see now, how can I ever repay you?" she asked.

"Huh, now that's worth the price, Nicki." He teased waking up fully as he took his wife in his arms and enjoyed all the benefits of his last day at home for a while.

Before long, Nicole flipped the covers back, turned off the atmospheric sleep screen with the sounds of the receding tide, and called to Martin. "Wheeew, I've worked up an appetite this morning, how about you?"

"Definitely! What's on the menu?" He asked, looking forward to one of Nicole's full-course breakfasts.

"Well, just to prepare you properly for your run, how about some green paste in a tube and then some white slime in a cup?" She replied, determined to let him know exactly what he would be missing at home. While he was chasing "sky gas", it certainly wouldn't hurt him to carry the memory of this morning along with him.

"Oh, here we go! Are we picking up where we left off the other day?" He asked, becoming a bit irritated by her ambush.

"I know, but this run seems to be bothering me more than all the others. It's really got me bugged, Marty!" She said, concerned about her feelings of dread at his leaving.

"You say that before every run, Nicki."

"I know, honey, but this time, I mean it. For this past week, I've had this unexplained tenseness, just this feeling Marty." She explained, trying to make him understand without alarming him.

"Maybe you just needed a good workout." He laughed, playfully smirking as he lifted himself up on one elbow.

"Stop it! I'm not kidding, Marty! Okay, for that, breakfast can wait until after I take my shower!" She stated in no uncertain terms.

"Oh, before I forget," Martin said, getting out of bed. "I'm meeting George and Joe Burwick at the center today for our pre-flight checks, and afterward we will be having dinner at the pilots' club. Did I tell you they assigned Star?" Martin called out, following her in the bath quarters as she ran steamy water in the shower. "That should make you feel better. It's a great ship, and I'm real familiar with how to handle her."

"Just keep in contact with us this time. It helps to let me know when you're in hibernation, so I don't wonder why you haven't." Reminded Nicole, as she opened the glass sliding panel and stepped into a waterfall of steam.

"Jeez Nick, you act like this is my first run. Can't you trust me?" he asked, a little more harshly this time. He really didn't have the patience for her premonitions this morning.

"Rather than sulking here at home today, why don't you join us at the pilot's club for a drink later? We should be done with everything by about 4:00 this afternoon," his conversation ending abruptly as he began brushing his teeth.

"Okay, be there with bells on!" she said, locking him out of her morning ritual and her continued worry about the run.

Martin was impatient to start the day. "I'm going to forego breakfast and take a shower at the club after my workout. See you later at the base, okay?" Martin quickly bids her goodbye before she could protest his early departure.

"Don't forget to call me. See you later!" She called out in an echoed voice above the calming waterfall of the shower.

* * * * *

Martin entered the base, this time heading straight for the pre-launch pad, hoping to find George and Joe at the Texas Star. There, they were checking out the gear to be loaded onto the shuttle later that day.

"How do we look, gentleman?" Asked Martin in mock seriousness as he approached them.

"We're missing a few safety items that the kid believes will be needed to meet OSHA requirements," George responded, as he looked up to Martin who was shaking his head in disbelief at any unnecessary delays that were being caused by a "go by the book" type of co-pilot. "No need to get pissed off Marty. I told you Joe's a real stickler for detail. Who knows, at some point during this run, I'm sure you'll be glad to have that quality along." He laughed, as he patted Martin on the back and went on with his work.

"How long have you guys been here?" Martin asked, directing his question toward Joe.

"We arrived about two hours ago, actually. I can't seem to find the gas filters or the array of masks we'll need, but here's a list of the missing items, including the filters and masks I just mentioned." Joe said as he handed his palm computer to Martin.

"I still prefer mine on paper, kid," Martin responded, with more disapproval in his voice than he intended. "Looks like a lot of equipment, here. We're going to use up all our profits in fuel just to get this puppy home, especially if you keep on adding to that list of yours. I'll tell you what, let's take only one of everything on the list and eliminate a lot of the unnecessary items." He said, sure that he would get some flak from the zealous new cadet.

"But sir, all of these items, in duplicate, must be included to keep us in compliance with OSHA!" Joe emphasized showing more attitude than he intended, as well.

"Yea, maybe so if we were going to Mars kid, but we'll be stopping at SOHOIII, so we'll let our destination govern our supplies list!" He instructed in a voice that broached no compromise.

"True, I hadn't thought of that. I suppose we could do without some of the extra heater's OSHA requires," Joe said looking a bit sheepish.

"It's okay, Joe, just don't throw your common sense out the window. Keep in mind though, OSHA officers usually don't have pilot training, and they don't understand the realities of flight. Oh, by the way, some of this gear was dropped off by the Agency to be delivered to SOHOIII. I agreed to play delivery boy, but we'll both benefit from a nice bonus in the end. What do you think?" He asked, realizing that fresh graduates were almost always looking to turn a buck.

Before Joe could respond, George broke in, "I was wondering what all that cargo was about, Marty. So, you found a way to work for the Agency after all, huh?" He joked, knowing the sarcasm would be returned.

"Just earning a living, my friend, but I suppose with your partial retirement you don't remember what it's like to have to hustle, do ya?" Martin commented in the same vein while pulling George aside. "What are you teaching these kids, anyway George? When we were flying, we weren't the least bit concerned with all this regulation shit!" He baited, waiting for George's return.

"Oh, you're showing your age now, Martin. Times, they are a changin'! Seriously, the government is beginning to really crack down on pilots, with all the crashes and disappearances going on lately," George said, knowing as well as Martin that the crashes and disappearances weren't due to the lack of safety equipment.

"Political! Somebody wants to look good by enforcing regulations, whether it helps or not!" Martin stated emphatically.

"Maybe but I have to teach by the book. That's why I'm relying on you to show these new cadets what it's really like out there in space. Some will adapt and some will fall by the wayside. Then, there are those who will be easy pickings for the 'sky cowboys'! Their first run will be one run too many for that kind!" George said, more to himself than anybody in particular. "You know, Marty, it's getting harder and harder to tell who's cut out to be a runner." George continued, turning to observe Joe who was still focused on checking his list.

"I know what you mean, George. They look like such babies, don't they?" Martin questioned, thinking to himself that he was able to totally relate to the challenges George faced with this younger generation. He often felt this way with Lance, uncertain whether he would be able to cut it in a man's world. "Well, I'm going to check out the cargo bound for SOHOIII. The Agency has provided the equipment list, but I want to make sure they haven't tried to pull a fast one on us. You know, include a few extras along the way that they're hoping we'll miss in our check." At that point, Martin began opening unlabeled crates.

"Joe," yelled Martin. "Why don't you and George take your needs list to Helen in the administration building and she'll do an update for you. Ask her to pay special attention to the safety equipment if it'll make you feel better." He said, jokingly. However, Joe felt the sting of Marty's sarcasm and was eager to get the hell out of there before he was tempted to show his anger.

"Now, let's see here," Martin said to himself as he opened the next crate, "Where is our Gas Chromatograph? Okay.... now..." he continued talking to himself as he methodically rummaged through one crate after another. Over the years he had learned to listen to that little voice that told him when something was not quite right, and he was hearing it now. He just couldn't put his finger on what it was that nagged at him, making him want to recheck all the SOHOIII station crates. Perhaps it was just the fact that, having dealt with the Agency for almost 20 years, he realized they often tried to pawn off cargo on him, materials no other runner would agree to carry. With all these strange items that Gila requested, he couldn't identify some of the equipment and that concerned him.

It's not that Martin didn't trust Gila, in fact, he looked forward to seeing his friend in SOHOIII station again. The issue was that the biosystems thought differently. Gila's priorities were in many ways very alien. Martin had never met a more purposeful and dedicated genetically designed life-form before, but then why shouldn't Gila be that way? Gila had been specially created to be the caretaker of the SOHOIII Station. Martin shook his head as he thought of the diverse variety of genetically designed life forms that science was able to successfully create by crossing plant and animal DNA each one having specific tasks that had contributed to Earth's far-reaching space explorations. They called these genetically manufactured beings, biosystems.

The biosystem debate was forever on-going. They are sentient, but at the same time, they were designed with a purpose in mind and from what Martin had seen they lived to fulfill that purpose. Biosystems were impossible to mass reproduce. Each one was unique and took decades to grow from genetically mutated cell lines. The cost to create one was substantial. Some more radical groups out there are always petitioning for biosystem rights while others petition for their destruction. The doomsday preachers who predict that the hubris of man's foray into the realm of God will be our downfall versus the bleeding-heart activists that crusade for the rights of biosystems as a people. The strange thing was that both sides of the coin were correct in their own way. The biosystems are not human.

Their reactions and instincts do not parallel ours and their concepts of happiness or "contentedness" we do not fully understand. They are so specifically designed for the environments they are supposed to endure, that even if the biosystems wanted a different life somewhere new, they would likely find it uncomfortable, at least for some transition period. Each biosystem is the main player of its own study. Socially-physically-habitually, we work with them and watch them as they, in turn, learn from us. The main topic at hand being their humane treatment, which all regulation concerning the biosystem projects have seemed to ensure.

Gila was one of the most sophisticated biosystems. He had large substantial photosynthesizing areas while heavily armored scales covered most of his body. Photosynthesizing surface allowed him to produce his own oxygen and the heavy armored plates. The scientists had provided helped to shield Gila from the incredibly intense bursts of radiation that came from being next door to the sun. Yeah, you could say that Gila was perfectly designed. He had great tolerance for high temperatures, low humidity, and could be exposed to high levels of radiation for an unlimited time without feeling any ill effects. Unlike humans, Gila could handle the emotional challenges of being absolutely alone for months on end.

Martin continued to sort through another SOHOIII crate, noticing an unusual array of clippers, plant food, linens, and books. Besides, it was a crate containing a large supply of people food, an assortment of catalog items ordered through the internet, which seemed to be various equipment parts and oil products. Martin didn't stop his search until he felt all was in order.

Having inspected the inventory, Martin's next task was to supervise the loading process onto the actual shuttle, then he could seal off the ship prior to launch, ensuring that he would be the only one aboard until liftoff. Martin walked over to the signal panel, and speaking to a dockworker, said, "You can begin loading now."

"You want all these items loaded and sealed tonight, sir?" The worker questioned, careful to please the Agency's runner.

Realizing that loading these items would mean the workers staying overtime and Martin holding up cocktails at the club he replied, "No, these can be taken aboard tomorrow," pointing to some of the items that Joe wanted to be added. The loading was a slow process, taking tedious hours to complete. All items had to be stored in secure locations to prevent damage during liftoff. While the workers loaded, Martin inspected the dozen collectors already on board to ensure proper operations of the containers when they arrived near a flare. Although some of the collectors showed wear and tear from previous missions, the electronics indicated no present malfunctions. The next half-hour came and went with Martin finishing the check on all the systems within the hydrogen collectors, and it was about this time that George returned from the administration building.

"I sent Joe on home to clean up before meeting us for a drink. Getting hungry Marty?" George asked.

"I'm starved. It seems I can't get enough food right before making a run. I guess it's because of my aversion to the crap they call food that we pilots are expected to digest in space," Martin said, enthusiastically. "I'll be cutting it close to four. Do me a favor and let Nicole know I may be a little late. I still have to instruct the ground crew to seal off the shuttle to everyone except me."

"Including Joe?" Asked George, with a tinge of concern in his question.

"Everyone!" replied Martin. "I'll okay the last-minute loading when those final supplies arrive, but otherwise, the ship is off limits!"

"Well, Joe's ready. He got all his papers signed and those supplies he wanted are due to arrive anytime. See you at the club then," he said, waving Martin off as he left the dock.

Martin couldn't help hoping that Joe was the pilot George promised he would be. It would be tough to send him packing once they left the Lunar Station. An alert popped up from his optical computer indicating that the dock workers were almost there with the last of the crates. "Thanks, guys, seal her up tight, OK?" Martin asked the exiting dock workers once they had finished their delivery.

"Done, sir. Have a good flight," the foreman replied.

As Martin left the Texas Star he glanced back, still confused by the trepidation he felt about this run. "Shit, Nicole has you spooked, that's all!" He said out loud to himself, as he was the only one around now. He was determined not to let these feelings spoil the building excitement of liftoff tomorrow. He wondered how many launches he would have to pilot before it felt routine.

* * * * *

The pilots' club was very luxurious and exclusive, but that was one thing Martin had come to accept as routine. He expected impeccable service, great food and the sights and sounds of his peers when dining at the club which specializes continental cuisine, and Martin was looking forward to his last dinner being one of the cook's famous concoctions. He glanced down at his communicator watch. "Not bad, only 30 minutes late," he said to himself. The chef looked around, squinting until his eyes became accustomed to the dim lighting. Then he located everybody seated around a large round table in the corner, sipping on drinks and already enjoying the conversation.

Martin slid in next to Nicole and gave her a kiss in greeting. "The ship looks almost as beautiful as you, honey." He enthused, glad to see she was in a mood to party with his friends. "Hi kids, how was your day?"

Wendy answered her father immediately, offering a bit of news about her classes. Lance remained quiet, refusing to do more than quietly grunt his response.

"So, we're done? All my equipment arrived?" Joe asked, eager to make sure things were in order.

"Some additional cargo arrived, but to be honest, I didn't check it out item by item as with the other cargo. I did notice the masks, filters, and several spare equipment parts, though. Some boxes I simply stowed away without confirming the listing on the outside. Not to worry, Helen is so efficient, I'm sure she correctly ordered your requested list," Martin commented, waving over the waiter to take his drink order. "Has everyone ordered?"

"Nope, too much fun conversation. We couldn't concentrate on the menus, could we kid?" George responded playfully, nudging Lance on the bicep with his bony elbow.

"I'm not hungry," Lance said. He never ate much at his dad's farewell dinners.

"Lance, don't do this again. Let's have an enjoyable evening. I don't want scenes during my last night before a run, okay?" Martin said, assuming Lance was about to create trouble.

Lance clenched his jaw. His look was nearly identical to his mother's when she was biting back words. The next few minutes were taken up with Lance cleaning his lenses and trying to blend into the back of the booth in order to avoid the conversation. Wendy, on the other hand, dominated the conversation as she retold the story of her birthday adventures for the hundredth time.

"So, Joe, you're still interested in becoming a runner, huh?" Martin prodded. "That's why I'm here!" He replied excitedly, knowing that he was being offered a unique advantage on this run to learn from one of the best.

"Sounds like you're willing to learn but are you just as willing to take orders?" continued Martin.

"I'm willing to do what it takes to become the best I can be!" Joe started, noticing the disgust on Lance's face as he anticipated a confrontation with Martin.

"The only two people I've ever flown with have been just that the best: my classmate Al, and George here. You've got some pretty heavy boots to fill." Martin teased, as he encouraged everyone to pick up the menu and decide what they wanted to eat. Although it was early, everybody at the table knew that bedtime and rise-and-shine came early just before a run.

"Dammit, I hate to be around you right before a run. I always get the itch to come along." George said, excitedly.

"Oh no you don't, sweetheart. It may be glamorous for you pilots flying around out there in space, but for those of us who stay behind, it isn't a thrill, I can assure you. We worry every day," added George's wife, Rita. "You better telecommute to Nicole often, Martin. Seriously, you don't know what it's like cooling your heels at home all the time. It's rough!" She ended, looking at the tenseness on Nicki and Martin's faces, and fearing she had stirred up a can of worms.

Everybody made an effort to let that subject drop as George lifted his drink to the group and toasted, "Here's to a successful run! We'll make him behave, Nicki, or he'll have to answer to me when he returns. Besides Joe will be there to remind him, won't you kid?"

"What about your family, Joe? Do you have to put up with all this worry from them?" Martin asked. Joe took a quick drink hiding his discomfort behind his glass then quickly chimed in, "Oh, they worry some too, like everybody who loves you should. Running can be a dangerous lifestyle. That's why I'm looking forward to learning from the best!" He brown-nosed, ready to pass the conversational ball to another easy target: Wendy. "So, you're sixteen now?"

He hardly got the words out when Wendy replied, in that flirting way only a 16-year-old has when she's trying to impress an older man, "Yeah, but I'm bored with my friends. They are such children!" She said in her pseudo-sophisticated voice.

"Bullshit, Wendy. You're the worst of the bunch!" Lance said, taking his aggression and frustration out on his sister.

"Lance! That's enough. What is your issue tonight? Not enough wins on those stupid computer games?" Martin found himself asking, trying to tease over the blowup, but he couldn't help revealing his aggravation at the constant anger that Lance showed toward the family, himself in particular.

Lance's jaw dropped. "Martin..." Nicole started, but was interrupted by her son, "I'm not the one being completely annoying!" Lance said turning to his mom. "Mom, you said I could go over to Doug's house for our school project tonight. He lives two blocks away can I go now?"

She glanced at Martin who flush a little from anger and a little from letting that anger get the better of him. Lance was hovering dangerously between tears and righteous 14-year-old-fury. "Lance, let's finish dinner. We're spending tonight with your dad."

"But mom, just for a little bit! His mom said she would bring me home after we were done," his voice had jumped about two octaves.

Nicole sighed, "Well alright, but don't get home too late. Let me drive you, sweetie," and turned to grab her purse as she started to get up.

Lance jumped up ahead of her, "No, I really just want to walk mom. I got my phone, but nothing will happen. It's a five-minute walk."

Nicole looked to Martin for help. Martin trying to understand his son in this moment, grabbed Lance's arm as he turned to walk away, "He'll be fine Nicole, give him a little independence. Lance, I'm sorry son. I'm going to miss you while I'm gone." Lance surprised him by throwing his arms around his dad in a big hug. His glasses were starting to get a little misty. "Love you dad." he mumbled.

"We'll talk later at home." Martin said hugging Lance back. With a mumbled "Okay" Lance turned wiping his eyes as he walked out of the dining room. Joe watched the boy go, a look of frank concern on his face.

After the initial discomfort created by Lance's departure, everybody busied themselves with their meals. Soon the conversation flowed smoothly again, and the scene seemed forgotten by the time Lance called to say he'd reached Doug's house just fine.

Dinner was perfect. Everything a man about to go to space needed. "I'm stuffed. Ready to go, girls? It's getting late," Martin glanced at his daughter and wife for confirmation. "Be here bright and early Joe, or I leave without you. We are to be suited up and ready for liftoff at 6:00 a.m."

"I'll be here probably before you, sir!" Joe promised.

"Good luck, my friends. Have a safe run and teach my cadet well!" George instructed, feeling the bite of one too many alcoholic beverages. "Joe, watch over the old man. He'll try your patience to the max!"

"Come on George; it's time for this one to go home!" Rita laughed, as she gave his arm a tug in the direction of the door. "Have a good run, Martin. We'll watch over everything while you're gone."

"Thanks, Rita!" He was about to say he was looking forward to it, but he didn't want to stir up any emotions in Nicki. Any more than Lance had done earlier in the evening, that is. He dreaded the confrontation they would have when he got home.

But conversation slowed in the transport on the way home. Wendy was asleep in the back, and Nicole's eyes were getting heavy.

In a way, Martin was glad to have his thoughts to himself. What would he say to Lance when he got home? That was the trouble, he always seemed to say the wrong thing. They were miles apart in their likes and beliefs, and the older Lance get, the deeper and more apparent the division. He loved his son, but he wasn't sure he would ever be able to understand him.

When Martin got home, he immediately went to Lance's door to get the drama over with so he could get a good night's sleep. To his surprise, Lance was curled deeply into the covers, snoring to beat the band. Maybe the disturbance wasn't all that big a deal. He would telecommute a private message to him since Lance probably wouldn't be up to see him off.

* * * * *

Morning came all too quickly as Martin found himself caught in the excitement of the Texas Star's liftoff. Joe's prediction had been accurate: he was already suited up and ready to go by the time Martin arrived. Just a few minutes passed before the pre-launch alarm blared throughout the dock. Marty and Joe made their way to the elevator just in time to be helped aboard the shuttle. He looked for the last crates that had been loaded on that morning, making sure they were secured-and they had. Looked like Joe had gone through a few of them to verify their contents, and he chuckled inside at his "old hen" behavior.

Once inside the shuttle, all they could do was sit and wait for instructions. As expected, Joe was doing last minute checks, and Marty had to admit he was getting a new appreciation for his cadet's expertise. But Martin was not to be distracted in this one moment of complete joy-total immersion into the glory of liftoff. It was this moment that never failed to exhilarate him.

"So, kid, how're you feeling? Pretty heavy stuff here, aren't it?" Martin teased, excited himself to be on another run.

"It's incredible!" Joe replied, short for words to express the emotions he was feeling.

"You think this is incredible now, wait 'til liftoff and your body parts are re-arranged. Your stomach in your throat, your heart beating at the speed of light, your ears ringing, head pounding and eyes pressured until you worry they're going to pop right out of your face!" Martin laughed, having fun with the discomfort he saw traveling up Joe's face.

In just a short while the control panel lit up and clearance was given for countdown. "Ten, nine, eight... one. Ready for blast off Texas Star!" The controller acknowledged.

"No turning back now, Joe. We're riding off into the sunset!" Martin said, doing his John Wayne impression. The last of his words were lost, though, by the activity of liftoff. Joe didn't seem to mind much; his thoughts at this moment were on survival and keeping down last night's dinner.

Nicole, Wendy, Rita and George watched the picture-perfect takeoff. Lance's absence was obvious to his family, but not wanting to stir up a hornet's nest on the morning of liftoff they ignored his disappearing act.

"Nice launch! How about we take a walk over to the officers' club? My treat!" Asked George in an attempt to ease worry.

"Maybe later, George. I need to get Wendy to school and hunt Lance down." Nicole said, not knowing where to begin to bridge the canyon that was eroding Lance and Martin's relationship. "I'll call you later. Don't worry about me. I'm fine, really, I am." She stated, but George and Rita weren't fooled by her brave face and staunch attitude. In a way, George was glad that Lance's behavior would distract her from her own loneliness and worry in the approaching week.

"Okay, I'll drop by tonight for just a moment when you telecommute with Martin. We'll go for dinner, and I won't take no for an answer!" George comforted her, anxious to see the return of Nicole's easy smile.

"You know me too well. Okay, I'll be needing a break from myself by then. Thank you both for your understanding. I love you guys!" Nicole choked, feeling herself tighten as she quickly hugged them both, then headed for her transport.

George wished he could do more for Nicole, but he had little time to linger before his class of new recruits arrived today for their introductory jolt of what running was really like outside the pages of their instruction manuals and the four walls of their classrooms. He took a moment to give thought to Lance.

"Where was the boy?" George thought to himself, concerned that he could at least have showed up for his dad's liftoff.

George was unaware that Lance had shown up for the liftoff, tucked away in a far corner of the ship where nobody would discover him until it was too late to do anything about it. He was proud of the way he had sneaked past the dock workers into a crate they loaded that morning. It had been much easier than he expected going straight from the pilot's club. "He'd show his dad how much of a man he was if it killed him!" Lance thought to himself, as his small frame was thrown about the supply closet. He escaped his fear by thinking about his clever cover-up last night and this morning. He had planted a wireless speaker in a pillow in his bed and rigged his computer to play sounds of snoring for most of the night so his dad wouldn't come in to wake him. "I'm officially a genius," he congratulated himself in a whisper. "Now all you have to do is stay in one piece, keep your food down, and enjoy the ride," he said again, wondering if his dad was right and he was nothing but a wimpy wire-head, unsuited for running. "No, you're not! You're a warrior!" Lance told himself, repeating the words of his favorite virtual reality hero! "Space here I come!"

CHAPTER 3

UNEXPECTED CARGO

Once the Texas Star was out of Earth's gravity, Marty looked over at Joe and started to laugh. "Not quite like the simulator, eh kid?"

"I feel like a martini that's been shaken but not stirred." Joe responded once he was able to talk.

"A launch is like the reverse of the birthing process. Instead of going from the tranquility of the mother's womb into the turmoil of birth, the shuttlecraft goes from a chaotic launch into the stillness of space. Then you just float with the serenity of being wrapped and protected in the loving arms of space, as it surrounds you and makes you feel as though you've just come home again," Martin said, and Joe could hear the absolute love of running in his eloquent speech.

* * * * *

Two days of hiding had taxed Lance's patience to the nth degree. He was fed up with being stuffed inside a closet not big enough to fit the smallest of biosystems, much less a growing young man who needed his space. He had to limit his movement to nights, rummaging for food in the galley and using his suit tubes to eliminate his bodily wastes. He could hear the increased excitement of his father and Joe's voices as they neared the Lunar Station. He was hoping to be able to escape for a day's adventure before going back into hiding. He couldn't afford to reveal himself until at least a week into the journey. That way he could be assured his father would refuse to turn around and take him home, knowing that the mission would have to be aborted for an entire year. "Just a few more hours until you can explore, old boy." Lance said to himself, unconsciously adopting the language of his father.

* * * * *

"You know, we're just two days out and our food supply is dwindling like crazy. I've got to give it to you Joe, your excitement hasn't decreased your appetite any." Martin called to Joe from the galley as he searched for a snack tube.

"What are you talking about, you don't see me at the galley every minute do you? In fact, you know I've not been there as much as you have," Joe retorted, defending Martin's accusations that he was being a pig!

"Kidding, Joe! Joke, it's a joke." Martin returned, but in reality, he was surprised at how their food supplies had diminished in such a short time. They would have to stock up at the station if they were to have enough for the long journey to SOHOIII.

Soon their destination came into view, in all its' splendor. It was a giant cylinder of units. Appearing to travelers as a bigger-than-life metal erector set with a hollow core that could not be seen from the outside. To reach the station itself, pilots were required to pass through a tunnel, or portal of sorts, to arrange themselves in various docking bays on the inside circumference. "Like a huge donut." Martin thought to himself. The two days away from home was already telling on his lust for real food.

"Jesus, is there no end to the size of this monster!" Joe questioned. He felt as though the entry portal was sucking them into another planet, a place where pilots could lose themselves in the anonymity of hundreds of others much like them.

"They keep adding units to accommodate the high traffic at this station. Wow, I can't even believe how much it's changed in just the four short years since I last saw it!" Martin exclaimed as he looked at their surround screens at the view unfolding before them.

"Amazing!" commented Joe, whose expectations were more than met by the wonder before him. "How many people actually live here on a permanent basis?"

"Let's see, several biosystems, but most of the people are scientists, up here temporarily, while working on some experiment or on some grant to study a particular phenomenon. I hear that some experiments on this Lunar Station have been on-going studies for the past decade. Most of the traffic you see now though, are pilots and runners using the station to refuel and relax." Martin stated matter-of-factly. "Quite a mixture of individuals, wouldn't you say?" He asked, knowing that Joe would be awestruck at the many different cultures, beings, and personalities on display inside the station, with runners tending to be the more worldly type.

"Do you feel capable of docking this thing, Joe?" Martin asked, wondering at his skills learned in the simulator and the few trips George required of his new cadets.

"If it's anything like the simulator, I've done it hundreds of times," answered Joe, naively.

"Reality, I'm sure you've experienced by now, can be a whole lot different from textbook running. If you're up for it, though, I'm willing to let you give it a shot," Martin said, remembering his first attempt at docking.

"I'm game," Joe said, placing himself in the ready position as they approached the portal. "We have a communication coming in from the station." Joe noticed, temporarily distracted from his attempt at getting behind the wheel.

"Oh, they should be expecting our arrival. Helen should have already gotten us clearance if she did her job correctly," Martin reassured Joe. "She has never let me down before!"

"Texas Star, you have clearance to dock and come aboard. You will be docking at slip 1355C. Welcome! Smooth docking, Texas Star. Over!" Apollowalla ended in her typical fashion, short and screechy.

Joe jumped back from the console, shocked at the strangeness of the voice he had just heard on screen. "Ever met a biosystem before Joe? Because you're about to," laughed Marty, after seeing Joe's reaction to the unusual voice.

"Do they all sound like that?" Replied Joe, staring at the console.

"Let me tell you. It pays not to insult them. Someday they may mean the difference between life and death in these environmentally controlled stations. And, you know what? If the shit hits the fan, they'll still be walking around long after everyone else is unconscious or incapacitated. In fact, they are known to be far more reliable than a computer when it comes to making life or death judgment calls!" Martin advised. "Joe, I want you to be prepared for whatever is ahead, and, by the way, wipe that shocked expression off your face when you're inside the station. It labels you as the new kid!"

"Ever since I heard of the biosystems I've wanted to meet one. I hear they're practically aliens," Joe commented.

"You'll know one when you see their green hair, which is where most of their photosynthesizing abilities come from. They will also be wearing a lighted helmet, which of course is a necessary ingredient for photosynthesis to occur. Up here, you'll grow to appreciate their symbiotic relationship with man when you need the clean air they produce as they absorb the carbon dioxide we put out. When you think about it, these transgenic beings have inherited the best of both worlds, be it plant or animal," added Martin.

"Rather convenient of us to create life forms that can survive in environments that are too harsh for humans to stand," mumbled Joe, still in awe of his first encounter with the space station as he continued to look out the glass panels surrounding two-thirds of the front of the Texas Star. "It's like evolution on fast-forward!" Clearing his head of amazement, Joe looked down at the panel of controls, instructing Martin in his most efficient cadet voice, "Hand her over, and be prepared to be dazzled!"

"Okay, I'll talk you through it the first time. Remember in the beginning to rely more heavily on your instrumentation than on what may appear outside the viewer. I found that it's difficult in space to judge distances or speed without much in the way of perspectives to aid you. Objects may be closer than you think, and your speed may be much faster than you've calculated. This is based on my experiences observing first-time dockings by neophytes!"

Martin joked, attempting to ease the pressure he knew Joe must be feeling by now as they queued in front of the docking portal.

"Thanks, any other wisdom you'd care to share?" Joe responded, secretly appreciating Martin's attempt to lighten the mood.

Martin began switching various stations in preparations for handing the helm over to Joe. "Ready to bring her in?" He asked, again eager to see what Joe could do.

Joe took control of the ship, but it wasn't without the natural hesitation and fear to be expected from a rookie. "When you move through the portal, you'll want to go to your right in the direction of slip 1355C," Martin instructed, pointing at the map that Apollowalla had provided on the screen. "That portal is a welcomed sight to many runner when it signals the end of a long and lonely space journey. You'll probably feel it too when we return."

To Martin, there were few man-made things as beautiful as the lunar station's docking portal gates. Their significance had been imprinted on him from nearly twenty years of running. He kept his thoughts to himself though as they passed through the tunnel since he knew Joe would not yet understand.

The defenses and security of the lunar station had not been a part of the original plans. Altercations occurring in space did not begin to occur until around twenty years ago when Martin had begun running. Space travel technology had always been kept under strict lock and key by the government organizations and corporations at the forefront of space exploration. Even today, space missions were not considered commonplace, making the concept of space banditry extraordinary. The shear lengths in resources and ingenuity for rogue space runners to stand a chance were staggering. One thing was for sure; any space pirate likely had a hell of a story to tell and probably had some interesting backers. The docking portals were an integral part of the defensive perimeter of the lunar station. The armory on the station was also a concept of much debate but overall was seen as necessary by the international consortium that governed the decisions regarding the station.

A proximity alarm triggered as the ship drifted too close to the tunnel's right wall. "Remember to watch your instrumentation, Joe,"

Martin warned, aware of a familiar nervousness, much like the one he experienced when he first taught Wendy how to use the transport. "Steady now!"

"My God, I've never seen anything like it!" Joe shouted in his enthusiasm for the adventure unfolding before him.

Martin was distracted by the speed of the Texas Star as she entered the inner core. "Stay to your right, Joe. With the traffic at this station, you never know when another ship is going to come around the corner to meet you head on. Okay, that's better," he said slowly. "Once you're inside the docking arena, rotate up to the third level before veering to your right. That should put us directly in front of our slip." Martin continued, not sure how he liked being the proxy navigator.

"Roger that," replied Joe, tensely concentrating now on piloting the Texas Star through the tunnel and readying her to spiral up immediately as they opened through to the inner core of the space station. "Jesus God!" There was that shocked expression back on Joe's face as he witnessed literally hundreds of ships going in directions which seemed to have no rhyme or reason, their lights providing a strange sort of laser show.

"Okay, there's our slip." pointed Martin. As the Texas Star entered the docking area, the individual bays were clearly distinguishable, even though the majority of the slips appeared to be in use. Martin's voice got a bit heated when he noticed Joe bringing the Texas Star too quickly to her right, knowing they would fall short of their slip and create all kinds of shit with the ships stacking up behind them. Martin was trying to hold his raveling nerves together, as Joe carefully followed his instructions, refusing to take his shouts personally.

"Great job, kid. I got to admit, you had me going there for a minute. Don't tell the world, but you did a sight better than I did during my first time out." Martin said, hoping the information would settle Joe's nerves as well.

"I suppose the docking could have been smoother, but I won't tell if you don't, sir!" Joe laughed, relieved at the release of all that pent-up stress since they had entered the docking area.

Just about the time Martin leaned back in his chair to let Joe know that it would be a while before they left the ship, he was alerted to a suspicious, unfamiliar noise coming from the direction of the supplies closet. "What the hell...?" he said, straining to hear it again. He held his finger over his lips as he looked at Joe while he slowly walked around the partition to the closet. When he yanked open the door Lance fell out landing roughly on the toe of his boot.

"What the fuck are you doing here Lance?!" Martin couldn't believe that his worst nightmare turned out to be a hundred pound 14-year-old boy in a pile on the floor at this very moment. "My God, this is some kind of joke. I know it. I'm going to have to take you back home and abort this entire mission because you've got some fool notion in your fuckin head. Stand up this instant!" he yelled, rattling the walls of the ship with his temper.

Killing the engine, Joe came back to investigate the commotion. "Lance! Oh my God, how have you managed stuffed in that closet for two days?" he said, trying to appease the boy's quaking fear of his raging father. "Come here. Are you hurt? Let me see."

"Don't baby the boy, Joe!" Martin ordered. "You're in deep shit, you little...." Martin scolded as he marched him to the main room of the ship. "How am I going to explain this to the Agency. Better yet how are you going to pay for the expense of this aborted run?" Martin questioned, running his hands through his disheveled hair, staring down at Lance in a fit of anger. "Lance, do you even understand? I could lose my pilot's license for this."

Lance had still not uttered a word, not ever having seen his father this upset with him, he didn't know what to do or say so he looked appealingly to Joe for a quick rescue. "Now Martin, this doesn't necessarily mean we'll have to abort, does it? I mean, he's made it this far. Couldn't we just take him to SOHOIII and leave him there in Gila's care while we collect the Hydrogen?" Joe asked, concerned for himself at this point.

"Absolutely not! I'm so damned mad, I could spit bullets. Not to mention, Joe, that it's against your famous regulations! We don't have the room or supplies to keep him aboard! Dammit, your mother must be worried sick! You have outdone yourself this time, boy, just outdone yourself!" Martin said disgustedly as he turned from his son, trying to figure out a way to handle this without having to abort. The first thing he thought of was to call Apollowalla, perhaps she'd have a viable resolution.

"Let's go check in with Apollowalla at her control center, and I'll telecommute to Nicole that Lance is here with me.'" Martin turned toward his son, firmly pointing his finger in his face and saying, "You sit your little ass right here and don't you move a muscle until we return. Maybe we send you back on another ship, I don't know, but if I can that's exactly where you'll be this time tomorrow bound for home and in a whole truckload full of trouble!"

"Dad, wait! I could be...!"

Lance didn't get a chance to finish his plea, his dad's look stopping him dead in his tracks. "You have nothing to say, son! Your only hope is to do nothing else to get in my way. Do you understand?" Martin said, clenching his teeth at Lance.

Lance mumbled something in return but didn't retort with his usual challenge to his father's authority. "Joe, go check the crates in storage A. I'll check the ones in B. Let's make this quick, so we can check in and get this mess sorted out." Then he pointed an angry finger at Lance, "And don't get cute with the computer!" Martin barked before disappearing to the back of the ship.

* * * * *

"Yes, sir." Lance replied, with a sour expression. Unwilling to admit it to his dad, he was determined to see SOHOIII, even if it meant stowing away on another transport and meeting them there. Getting up and sitting at the computer console, he ignored his father's warning, as he busied himself with "Plan B".

"Okay, first things first," Lance said in a whisper as he began exploring avenues in the computer. It didn't take him long to make a realistic looking hologram that reacted to heat and sound. "Oh, this could be good!" he continued, rigging the computer image to turn in the direction of approaching heat or sound vibrations. His finishing touch was the coolest, however, knowing it would be what fooled his dad into believing he was still sitting right where he should be when he was long gone. He made its expression turn to one of a pouting, angry attitude, then it grunted one of his usual replies to his father's sarcastic remarks. "Perfect, Lance, you're a genius!"

Checking his image from a distance, Lance was impressed with his handy work. He couldn't afford a moment longer to admire it though as he heard Joe and his father approaching from the collector's storage area. "... you bet I will!" Lance hid around the corner to the ship's entrance, laughing to himself as he saw his father speak to the computer image. "We'll be back by nightfall, and you better be here!" Martin warned. As planned, the image turned its head in his direction, gave a grunt, and leaned its head, bored like, over on the console top.

It was like watching himself. Very cool! For the first time, Lance was happy his father didn't realize the extent to which he had investigated every computer in sight. Now he could take his time exploring the station, making alternate plans in case his father didn't let him ride to SOHOIII.

CHAPTER 4

EXPLORATION

Martin and Joe made their way to the front "desk" for check-in with Apollowalla and to seek her advice on what to do with Lance. "Let's check into our berths. I hope to God she's got an extra one available for that kind of mine. Jesus! He pisses me off. Why the hell would he do such a stupid thing?"

"Maybe he really loves space!" Martin's frown registering that Joe's joke was not particularly funny. Joe was still getting to know Martin. It wasn't exactly a spoken rule, but prying into the personal business of anyone you were going to be spending a large amount of time with, in extremely dangerous and CLOSE quarters was paramount to disaster. Drama in space could result in true misery for everyone involved. Maybe it was the relative "breath of fresh air" granted by the lunar station, or maybe it was just that Joe really kind of liked Lance, but Joe was feeling brave. And hey, if his insight could help a father and son connect, then score one for the team of misunderstood boys everywhere. "I thought it was pretty clever of the kid. I'd be interested in how he did it. Although it doesn't say much for the Agency's security if they can be outsmarted by a fourteen-year-old," Joe took Martin's non-committal grunt as encouragement to continue. "I still can't believe he essentially lived in that closet for the entire trip. Think Apollowalla would make him an appointment at the hospital bay?"

"He seemed fine, Joe."

Joe noticed the red flag coming from Martin's tone and knew he'd need to proceed carefully. "Ya, he did, didn't he? It just kind of looked like he might have been playing it tough, you know, maybe trying to impress his old man," Joe's side-long glance watched Martin's profile carefully.

For a minute, neither man spoke. Joe's thoughts revolved around the complicated history with his father or in his particular case, fathers. Although, realistically Joe never considered his stepdad as much of a father figure. More like the bully who taught him a few of life's less-than-pleasant-lessons at a young age.

"As soon as we talk to Apollowalla, I'll call Nicole and we can map out our plan from there." Joe had the distinct feeling that the "we" Martin was referring to did not include him. "Oh, and don't forget what I said about pissing off Ms. Apollowalla. The last guy who did called her a freaky vegetable woke up with a Christmas cactus growing on his ass."

"Can we get something to eat, besides toothpaste after that?" asked Joe.

"Sure. The Lunar Café is one of the best in the Solar System."

As they walked down the main corridor, which was suspended in a magnetic field. Joe could barely contain the sounds of appreciation that escaped his throat. "Man, this place is amazing," he said. The closeness to the other planets in the solar system brought a surreal look to the place. Venus seemed close enough to touch, while Mars loomed in the distance, seemingly oblivious to the fact that there were other planets. And earth, the most beautiful of all, splendid in its brilliant blue looked back at them longingly.

"Here we are." Martin broke the silence.

Joe looked at the sight before him and tried his best to seem unaffected. The creature at the control desk looked like a big stalk of celery with eyes and a space helmet full of green hair. Her arms performed multiple tasks and she spoke into a tiny headset that was built into the tremendously large helmet. Her eyes were bulging and perfectly round, like those of a goldfish. And yet, her lips were definitely feminine. Joe could not believe that anything on this thing could look like a woman, but those lips! He found himself swallowing hard to choke back a gasp. Martin did the talking.

"Hello, my dear Apollowalla," he said, placing a beautifully potted plant on her counter.

"How lovely! I adore this species." She screeched, obviously taken in by Martin's gift. "It's so great to see you, Martin. I wasn't sure if I would ever see you again. There were rumors that you were going to retire, and I know that lovely wife of yours is always trying to plant your roots in Earthen soil."

Every syllable was like nails on a chalkboard to Joe. "My God," he thought to himself, "if they all talk like that, I'll be mad before we take off."

"I'm not retiring just yet. I'm not ready to sit around and watch image master for the next forty years. I'm glad you like the plant sweetheart. Just a little show of appreciation from this old pilot," Martin said winking charmingly at the biosystem. "Ms. Apollowalla let me introduce my new trainee, Joe Burwick."

"Hello," mumbled Joe, doing his best not to look right into those buggy eyes.

"Nice to meet you," she answered back. "I have a berth reserved for you Martin, and your companion's berth will be just around the corner. Is that acceptable?"

"Ummm, I have a slight problem that I was hoping you could help me with. You see, unbeknownst to me, my son, Lance -- you've seen his pictures -- stowed away on our ship. I don't want to abort the mission, but there's very little else I can think of to do. Do you have any suggestions for me?"

"Whew! That's a sticky one. Well, he could always stay here until you get back. His board fee wouldn't be that much. I could arrange a discount for you and possibly put him to work. I would also have to assign a biosystem to supervise him because he is under the required experience age. The bio-nanny I have in mind is wonderful. He gets along with everyone and although he's getting up there in age, he acts like a sapling much of the time. His name's Brendle. I'll get him for you if that's your choice."

"That's what we'll do, as long as Nicole goes for it." Martin said. "Oh, and speaking of Nicole, where did you move the telecommute center to?"

"Just down the hall from your berth, in section 6B. Here, take the map. This place has quadrupled in size since you were last here."

"Thanks. I'm going to call home as soon as I can find my way there. Joe, go check on Lance, will you?"

"Sure Martin." Joe said turning to start back towards the ship. Personally, he was still concerned that Lance could be hiding some injuries from the take-off. A couple of Joe's ribs were sore from where the buckles had over tightened during the blast off. He didn't know how Lance secured himself, but he highly suspected the boy would be more willing to confide in any problems with Joe than he would with his father. His father might be hard on him, but Joe knew better. The boy just needed a little understanding and hey, Joe was only twenty-two, and he knew a thing or two about difficult fathers. Joe was pretty much the epitome of the perfect role model for the boy.

He entered the ship and was a little surprised to see that Lance was still sitting at the computer console where they had left him. Lance looked up as Joe approached. "Hey Lance! So, how's your first trip to space treating you?" Lance just continued to look at him, his face morphing into a fairly impressive sulking pout. "Well, OK, could be better I see..." Alright, so maybe Lance wasn't just going to immediately pull Joe into his inner circle of personal thoughts. "So, uh, I was thinking about heading over to the hospital bay. I have a couple of bruised ribs from take-off. Would you want to come with me?" Lance mumbled something that sounded like a "no". "Oh, well great then. Want to head over to the Lunar Café for some grub?" Lance finally turned his back to Joe and just sat staring at the computer console. Joe scratched his head, maybe this kid was a little stranger than even he anticipated. "I'll just tell your dad you wanted to stay on the ship then. We'll bring you back something." Lance continued to ignore a completely stupefied Joe, who finally with an awkward goodbye turned to go find Martin at the telecommuter.

* * * * *

Martin passed by the docking area again on his way to 6B near the center of the lunar station. He was pleased to see the Kitty Hawk floating silently in its hanger. Martin made a mental note to touch base with his old friend Bill Harding. The Kitty Hawk was a small, yet durable little ship that Bill had built for his own independent use, rather than continuing to rent. Independent ships had the benefit of avoiding a lot of the bureaucratic process that slowed down planning a run. Bill could make the trips quicker and more efficiently, but the size of his vessel limited his haul. Martin hadn't heard much from Bill recently since his wife Carol had passed away. They didn't have any children and these days Bill seemed to spend more time on runs than on Earth. Sometimes he'd make a run and then turn right around to make another with only a week's break in between. Bill was a good man. He had been in the same training class as Martin and the two had become friends.

Just as he rounded the next corner, 6B loomed ahead. "Here we go," Martin announced to himself. He kept picturing Nicole panicked looking for her lost son. The thought made Martin shake his head at the selfishness of the stunt Lance had pulled. He took a deep calming breath as he entered the number for home and the link was instantaneous. "Hello honey!" he said, "You'll never guess who's here with me."

"Oh, I bet I could. Let me see. He's a boy, he's fourteen and he looks a lot like you." The image of Nicole on the telecommuter showed her in the kitchen. His eyes glanced to the knife that she had been chopping carrots with and was somehow using to intimidate him from 200,000 miles away.

"Nicole, baby... let me just say that I had nothing to do with this."

"He called me on the telecommute as soon as communication was possible, on board your ship. You should be so prompt!"

"What did you say to him? I hope you jumped his ass like I did!"

"I didn't Martin. He needs you. He needs this time with you. He's light years ahead of everyone in his class. He could miss quite a lot of school and still be ahead of the game. Talk to him Martin."

Martin shook his head. Now, he was really lost. He expected Nicole to step up to the plate and take his side. It just never occurred to him that he could be wrong. "Well, I can't take him with me to SOHOIII. The trip's too dangerous. I'm not going to take a chance where my son is concerned. My leafy friend, Apollowalla has agreed to let him stay here while I continue the mission and that's just what I'm planning to do."

"Martin I've never been to space, so I want you to make the call, but let me throw your own words back at you, it's perfectly safe. Do you remember telling me that? Do you remember how you promised me there was no danger? Well, in the words of my favorite renegade runner; shit or get off the pot, Martin. Is it safe or is it dangerous? If it's safe, take our son. If it's dangerous then you had no business going and risking our life together. You make the call."

God! He was pissed. She had no right! "Damn it, Nicole! It's not dangerous for a seasoned pilot but it could be for a kid. Don't you understand the difference? I can't be worried about wiping someone's nose when I'm trying to do my job! He's staying here and that's final!"

"You do what you need to do. I love you very much and I trust you, but you have to know that I, too, have a say so in our lives and I want this mission to be your last. I want you home for good this time. The destiny you're playing with so cavalierly isn't just yours. It's ours," Nicole's reaction startled Martin. He expected her to be upset and maybe that's what this was, but this wasn't an argument they have ever had while he was on a run. Calling home was always excited hellos and fervent updates that both of them needed to help them through their time apart. In a lot of ways, this felt like Earth Nicole was somehow usurping his time with his Space Nicole.

"I know, dear," Martin said, softening and reverting back to Earth Martin for this age-old argument of theirs. "I'll think about it. Get some sleep and I'll talk to you soon." Martin played many different roles on earth, father, husband, teacher, and friend. However, here in space, he was only one thing, a runner. A runner, no matter how dangerous a situation might become, who would return with his haul. He had discovered early on that home and work did not mix, especially when work involved running. Lance was definitely causing those lines to blur.

Just as they hung up, Joe appeared. "Knock-knock! Well, what'd she says?" he asked.

"She knew. She wants him to stay with us. I can't do that, though. You know how risky this can be. What did he say when you checked on him?"

"Uhh... he says he's not hungry and wants to sleep on the ship. He's gotten really comfortable there. I told him we'd pick him up something from the Lunar Café," Joe said as he looked everywhere but directly at Martin.

"Terrific. Thousands of miles away from home and he still isolates himself. Oh well, let's go get that food."

The two men walked for what seemed to be an hour, following the map that Apollowalla had given them. They passed an entertainment room for kids; something Martin noted that Lance might love. It made him realize that there were others who stopped here; not just runners. Families on vacation, scientists with their families and the employees who lived there made it a very large community. It amazed them both to think that they were just in one small hallway of a complex that was half the size of the moon. A large movie theatre showed the latest of films in any language in the solar system. There was a commissary for restocking supplies, a clothing store, and a large library. Martin was in awe at all the changes. They were about to turn the map upside down when they found the Lunar Station Café.

"Wow!" said Joe, "This place is huge."

He was right. The Lunar Cafe now stretched out over fifteen thousand square feet. There was a seating area for food, a dance floor, a bar that stretched seventy feet along the east wall, and an oxygen lounge area for relaxing and clearing the mind. The two men made their way over to the restaurant section of the giant room. The restaurant was manned by robots of all shapes and sizes that moved around the area quickly, taking orders and bringing food. "Good evening," said a small green creature with a neatly trimmed shrub for a head and a mass of flowers protruding from various parts of her body. She carried with her, two hand-held tablet menus. "You can search for specific entrees or if you would like to browse you can enter in a country or cuisine. We also have our specialties, which will automatically design a three-course meal based off of your current mood. In the meantime, can I offer you a cocktail?"

"I'll have a Gelatin Breeze," said Joe whose mouth was already watering at the thought of the thick Amaretto mixture.

"Just a beer for me, please," added Martin. He loved the idea that they had found a way to preserve his one indulgence. They had created a low atmosphere carbonation technique! He had to watch every line on his body since turning forty, but after today, he really needed a beer. Both men scrolled down the tablet to select their dinners. Joe selected a mixture of vegetables and steak while Martin chose a heavy cheese soup with a bagel on the side and a hamburger to go for Lance. The younger man quietly joked to Martin; "Do you think it freaks these biosystems out to see people eat a plate of vegetables?"

Martin responded, "Couldn't say but, in general, they show little concern for such matters. They just do their jobs and go about their way. There is one thing for sure. There are quite a few more since I was here last."

They gave their orders and then sat back to enjoy their drinks. Conversation between the two was light as they took in the sights around them and waited on their food. After a satisfying meal, Martin would take Lance his dinner while Joe would hang around for a while and take in the sights. They said their "goodnight" and then parted company.

The moment Martin and Joe had left the ship, Lance had slipped out for a little adventure of his own. His spirits were high from the success of his hologram, and it was time to see what wonders the lunar station held to entice genius boy Lance Mercer! He quickly pulled a map of the station up from one of the visitor directories and made his way to the Miakoda Gaming Complex described as, "The lunar station's premiere gaming, gambling, and dancing venue! Perfect for all ages!" The complex was made up of several floors, with floors 2-6 specified as ages eighteen and older.

Floor one was a complete bore. It had taken him one round on each machine to conquer the entire room. "Baby stuff", he thought, as he headed for higher ground. Loud bass was reverberating down from the upper floors where a line of people was scanning their IDs through an electronic access point being monitored by a seedy looking bouncer. The access point was likely verifying people's ages and then a sliding glass door would open to allow entry to the darkened lounge and dance areas above. Lance stepped up to glance through the doors and the bouncer grinned at him menacingly. Lance was not normally interested in this sort of establishment and having exhausted the potential of the first floor was turning to leave. The doors burst open as a couple of bouncers, hauling two very drunk and very young runners, came out. The runners were definitely enjoying hassling the bouncers. One of them had lost a shoe somewhere and the second one seemed to be pretending he could no longer walk. A tussle between the bouncers and the drunk runners broke out as the shoeless runner managed to propel himself off of the glass doors shoving the bouncer holding him into the wall. He was about to run back up the escalator when the bouncer from the entrance tackled him. All three bouncers were now escorting the two pilots out of the complex. With their backs turned to Lance, he had about one second to decide if he was going to make a break for it or not.

It was the strangest thing as he slipped through those glass doors, truly not a single thought passed through his head. He was almost surprised when he found himself slinking up the escalator into the darkened lounge. The lounge area was fairly crowded, and Lance stayed along the wall trying to blend into the background as he explored. He made his way over to some private booths and dove into one of the empty ones as the complex security on this level was patrolling nearby. "Great..." he thought as the security guard stopped in front of the entrance to the section forcing him to remain hidden beneath a table. Besides seeing some fairly R-rated dancing, he was starting to regret his little escapade when he keyed in on the muffled voices coming from the next booth over.

"Reg, he's late man. I don't like this shit," Lance could see a portion of the speaker's profile, a long scar ran down the left side of his face from mouth to ear partially covered by shaggy salt and pepper hair.

There was a slight pause before a deep resonant voice responded, "Give it another five minutes....and no names, remember we're in public."

"We should be long gone from here, bro. If that old man recovers or someone recognizes the ship we're boned," the man who Lance had mentally named "Scars" said to Reg.

At this point, Lance saw Scars get yanked across the table and out of view. "Shut... your... mouth...Do not make me say it again."

Lance wanted out of there. Who were these guys? No, what was he thinking? What would these men do if they saw him? He froze as a pair of legs stopped in front of his hiding place. A pair of steel-toed cowboy boots were pointing directly at the table with the two sinister men. "Hello gentlemen, sorry I'm late. I don't expect our business to be long, though. I assume the same terms as last time." Boots sat down in the booth across from its current occupants. The distance letting Lance release a long breath he hadn't realized he had been holding.

A light flashed near the private tables as a robot with a cleaning cart was making its way down the aisle efficiently cleaning the tables. It paused right in front of Lance's booth as it cleaned the area next to him. He edged his way out by keeping low, and managed to make it back to the crowded dance floor before the robot had moved on and exposed his back to the group of strange men. Lance was pretty damn spooked. He just wanted out of this place, but he hadn't thought that far ahead yet. There was no way he could go back the way he came. He glanced around and spotted a fire exit. The only issue is it was back at the end of the private tables, and he would have to walk past those dangerous men.

Lance kept his head down as he walked through the aisle. He couldn't help himself and looked up at the men as he walked by. Scars was dressed in nice, but rumpled clothing and looked as if he hadn't shaved in a while. The other man, Reg, was a smaller black man. He looked up and grinned at Lance as he passed by. Lance stared at his mouth where several of his teeth had been replaced with what looked like platinum. His dress was immaculate; white flowing garments held in place by well-tailored leather vesting. Both men had a look about them that made Lance cringe. They hardly noticed the young boy beyond pausing their conversation as he passed by.

Lance quickly made his way back to the Texas Star. He had to tell his dad about the two guys. But what would he tell him, really? Oh, I snuck into a club and overheard these guys talking when I was supposed to be back on the ship. I don't know what they were talking about but I'm sure it wasn't good. Yeah, right. He'd keep it to himself. What a crappy adventure.

Lance's relationship with his dad was a strange one. In one way, he admired his father, the well-respected hydrogen runner, the great adventurer. He could never see himself doing something like that for a living, however. On the other hand, he sometimes hated his father who was so good at making Lance feel like an embarrassment. Couldn't he see how smart Lance was? His ideas always seemed to bore his father. His mother would refer to them as her "Oil and water". Maybe Lance just wanted to prove that he had a little oil in him too. With that, Lance hurried back to the shuttle to replace the hologram with the real thing.

He'd barely shut down the image when his father stuck his head in and said, "Hey Lance, I brought dinner. How're you holding up?"

"Yeah, I'm fine. What are you planning on doing with me?"

"Well," said Martin, stepping up into the small room, "We've made arrangements for you to stay here until I get back."

"But Dad," Lance protested, "I wanted to be with you! I wanted to see SOHOIII!"

"I know son, but it's dangerous and I'm not risking your life on some crazy whims you have!"

"Please. Dad," Lance begged.

"No. It's not up for discussion. A biosystem is going to oversee you while we're gone. That's kind of cool, right? They're neat creatures. Apollowalla didn't have an extra berth ready for you, so you can go ahead and take mine tonight and I'll just stay on the ship."

"No dad. I'll stay here. I'll be fine... thanks," Lance said dejectedly. His dad would never listen. He'd never hear him.

Martin gave Lance an uncomfortable rub on the head. He didn't really know how to express his love to his son even though he knew he needed to. He turned and walked out the door, giving Lance one more glance and a "goodnight".

Martin walked slowly back down the corridor. He wasn't really that tired. In fact, he thought maybe he'd join Joe in the bar. The noises from the bar were decidedly louder than they had been earlier in the evening. Runners and workers were winding down their day and were now ready for some party time. As he entered the area, his eyes quickly scanned the bar for Joe. He found his co-pilot, and his attention went to the two companions that Joe was sharing a bottle of scotch with. Gully and Whiskey, two notorious runners.

All three runners looked up as Martin approached. "The legend himself! Long time no see Mercer." Gully said as he grabbed a new shot glass, filled it with scotch and set it down in front of the empty stool next to them. "Have a drink with us. Marty. Your co-pilot here was just telling us that he'll be graduating from the academy after this trip. We thought we'd toast to a virgin runner's first run."

Marty grunted as he sat on the stool. "Just a heads up, Gully, Joe's not worth robbing and you're not getting anywhere near our ship without going through me. Go find another target boys."

"Damn Mercer! We're just having a couple a drink with a new runner here. No reason to get your panties in a bunch, old man." Whiskey said grinning up at Martin as he downed another shot.

Martin ignored the two runners. Over the years, these two had picked one too many fights with friends of Martin's. It didn't usually mean he avoided them, but they would be a bad influence on Joe. If he were in a better mood, maybe he'd have stayed to have a couple drinks, but right now, knocking a few heads around might be a nice distraction and he didn't doubt these two were on the prowl to make that very thing happen. "Joe, I want to stop over at the Kitty Hawk and catch up with Bill Harding."

"Ya sure, Martin," Joe said. He pulled some cash out of his wallet and laid it on the bar. "I'll come with you. Thanks for the drinks, guys."

"Harding's not here man. His co-pilot, Graves just came through on a run. He mentioned Harding's grounded for the next few months while he finishes some upgrades on the Kitty Hawk. He's swapping over all the systems to the new Alpha OS. Have you seen that shit? All voice activation and the new interface is supposed to cut way down on the control lag time. Fuck! Whiskey, we need to get our own ship man, that's the way to go!"

Gully was reaching for the scotch again when Martin grabbed his arm. "Gully, are you drunk? I just saw the Kitty Hawk in the hanger."

Gully only shrugged as he looked at Martin. "I don't know, maybe he finished the upgrades early. Graves is probably pissed he took that other job then."

"Come on Joe. Have a good night getting into trouble boys," Martin said as he got up.

"Oh, we plan on it, Mercer! Good luck on your run, rookie. Don't let the old man completely choke you with that short leash of his," Whiskey said smirking at Joe.

Martin and Joe left the Lunar Cafe on their way towards the hangar where they had seen the Kitty Hawk. "You could probably have chosen better drinking buddies back there Joe. Gully and Whiskey are lively, but tonight wouldn't have been healthy for your reputation if you kept up with them. I'd keep it under wraps too, that this your first run. People get bored up here and some people see the naive as a form of entertainment."

Joe laughed lightly trying to keep the. "Is this guy for real" thoughts he was having from passing over his face. Instead, he responded with, "I hear you, Martin. I wasn't planning on going anywhere with those two. It was just a couple of drinks."

They passed the hanger and Marty glanced up at the Kitty Hawk. He could see some activity on board, so he thought he'd stop by and check out the situation. It was late, but someone was moving around in there.

"Hey there Billybob! You at home?" Martin hollered inside the door.

"Can I help you?" asked a stranger from inside.

"Oh, I'm sorry," answered Martin. "I thought Bill Harding would be aboard, with this being his ship and all."

"I rented it from him for a quick run." came the reply. As the body behind the voice came into view Martin thought he recognized the runner from somewhere. The scar on the left side of his face was impressive and was definitely ringing some bells.

"I wasn't aware that he ever let his precious ship out of his sight." Marty said to the stranger.

"Well, I guess he needed the money, and the wife wouldn't let him get away this time." Joked the stranger.

Martin knew something was up, now. Bill's wife had been dead for some time. "I didn't catch your name Mr..." Martin held out his hand in a friendly handshake.

The runner frowned but took Martin's hand, "Call me Vic."

"Name's Martin, nice to meet you, Vic. How are the new upgrades on the Kitty Hawk? I hear Bill just upgraded all the systems with the new Safe OS," Martin said.

The runner stared at him for a moment, "They're great. It was a solid investment." Martin felt Joe shifting feet behind him.

"Ya think so. I've always preferred Alpha myself. Well, if Bill's not around..." Martin's fist finished his sentence as he sent Vic to the ground clutching a broken nose. "Joe, go find something to tie this bastard up with."

"I think you should reconsider Joe. As an alternative I'd suggest putting your hands in the air and getting down on your knees," Martin and Joe froze as a man exited the ship aiming a gun in their direction. His ebony skin contrasting with his pure white suit. Both Martin and Joe slowly raised their arms. "On the ground gentlemen. Vic get up and get in the ship. We're leaving." Martin was glad that Joe followed his lead as he sank to his knees. He twitched his hand slightly pointing out the crates on their left. He hoped Joe's grunt was an indication that he understood.

Vic pulled himself to his feet. Martin doubled over as Vic's kick took him right in the ribs, "Mother fucker..." then Vic turned and climbed into the Kitty Hawk.

Guns in space were always stupid. There was never any point to carry something that could result in your death if you ever tried to use it for defense. Martin was still "clutching his ribs" as he pulled one of the small flash bombs that he tended to prefer from his chest pocket.

"Well, gentlemen. This is where we say goodbye," Vic aimed the gun at Martin's head and Martin threw the flash bomb. A gunshot went off as Joe and Martin dived for the crates. The black man was clutching his eyes as he took one step forward, then turned to dart into the ship. "Vic, get us out of here now!" Martin and Joe could only watch as the Kitty Hawk left the Lunar Station and took off into space.

CHAPTER 5

LANCE'S SOLUTION

Lance finished the food his father brought him then headed down to the docking bays to get a look at some of the ships. He had not been there long when he found his father and Joe running down the corridor.

"Dad!" exclaimed Lance as he ran up to them.

"Son! Listen! I need you to run up to Apollowalla's office and see what she can do to bring the Kitty Hawk back here. I need to get to a telecommuter."

Lance didn't know what was going on, he noticed what appeared to be a red stain expanding on Martin's arm, "Is that blood dad?!"

"Look at me Lance." Martin said as he grabbed Lance by the shoulders. "It's just a scratch. Right now, I need you to not ask questions and just do what I ask. Do you remember where the control office is?"

"Ya, I gotcha dad." Lance said breaking off into a run towards Apollowalla's office. Martin broke loose in the quickest run he could manage in the reduced gravity and reached 6B in no time. He was dialing Bill's number by the time Joe was at his side. The communicator rang. "Harding's residence."

"Is Bill there? Who's this?" Martin didn't recognize the voice on the other end.

"This is the house cleaning service. Mr. Harding isn't home right now. There was an accident and he's still recovering at the hospital."

"Shit... uhh sorry. Do you know which hospital?"

"No sorry sir. I wasn't told very much."

Martin said a quick goodbye and closed the link on the telecommuter. By the time Joe and Martin had made their way to the control office they found a wide-eyed Lance doing his best to answer the alien looking Apollowalla's questions.

"Hello, Mr. Mercer and Mr. Burwick," Apollowalla greeted them as they entered her office. "Security was already notified about the Kitty Hawk. Apparently, there was recent gunfire in that docking bay that they were responding to. I was just informing your delightful son that I find it unlikely that they will be able to retrieve the ship from space, but trackers have been launched and there is the possibility that the ship can be retrieved once it docks at its next location. Now, I will need your report concerning this incident if you two would have a seat," Apollowalla indicated two chairs off to the side of her desk. She quickly dialed a number from her telecommuter and a young girl with her dark hair in a ponytail and blue scrubs popped up on the screen.

"Nurse Joyce, could you bring a medical kit to my office. There is a gentleman here with a minor laceration. I anticipate four to eight sutures will be necessary."

There was a quick reply from the telecommuter and then Apollowalla clicked the screen off just as another person walked into the office. "Well timed Sergeant Wallace. This is Martin Mercer, his son Lance and Joe Burwick. These are the gentlemen who were present during the incident in Bay 24. I was about to listen to their report if you would like to ask any questions. Please have a seat."

The sergeant nodded to the men present in Apollowalla's office and turned on his optical computer that he wore above his ear. "Does anyone mind if I record this?"

"Umm, no," Martin replied a little taken aback by Apollowalla's efficiency.

Sergeant Wallace pulled up the recording of the events getting the details of the conversation that occurred between Martin and the man calling himself Vic. By the time the second ship thief appeared on the screen, Lance had jumped out of his seat, "That's them! Dad, I saw these guys at the entertainment center in sector 3."

"What? Lance when did you…" Lance interrupted his father. "Dad, I heard them talking! There's a third guy they were working with."

"Can you describe the third man Lance?" Sergeant Wallace turned to Lance who had begun to wilt a little under his father's scowl.

"His back was to me, but I saw his brown hair and a standard jumpsuit. But he was wearing cowboy boots! I don't think he was on the ship with the other two guys either."

"Why do you think that son? Also, can you tell me what time you saw these men at the entertainment center?" Sergeant Wallace continued with his questioning.

Lance blushed and started to stare at his boots, "Around four o'clock." He knew his dad had put two and two together. "I heard him say that he was interested in buying whatever they were selling is all."

"Alright, I'll get a team together. We'll see if this man is still on the lunar station and bring him in for questioning. Mr. Mercer are you and your crew going to be around for questioning in the next day or two?"

"Lance will, but Joe and I are leaving on our run in the morning."

Mr. Wallace nodded, "Alright, your clearance checks out Mr. Mercer. Lance if we locate the third man would you be willing to help identify him as best you can?"

Lance only nodded his response. Apprehension at the impending trouble he was in had glued his eyes to the floor.

"We're going to be doing a supply run to SOHOIII. If you could forward any information on the state of Bill Harding, I would appreciate it. He's an old friend."

Sergeant Wallace nodded as all the men in the office rose ready to part ways. "After this much excitement I am going to need an afternoon in the hydroponic lounge." Apollowalla said as she walked the men out of her office.

* * * * *

Martin had to prepare for his departure tomorrow but worried that the two unsavory characters Joe had been talking to might try to follow them and pirate their shipment. That sort of thing was happening more often lately. Just like the old days, of centuries past, the sailing ships were boarded, the crew subdued or in some It was common horrible incidents, murdered. The ships were then plundered and what was left over was given to the ocean. It was common knowledge that Gully and Whiskey were behind some suspected hijackings, but there was never enough evidence to revoke their cards. Martin had to make sure that he and Joe got a head start on those two. Life was easier when he soloed his runs, now an uneasy feeling began to creep over him, a feeling that he was starting to get used to on this particular run.

He quietly got up from his berth; sleep rarely came easily to him the night before a big departure and walking around the station might help. Martin still had not gotten a chance to speak to Lance. He had gone straight back to the ship while Martin had been delayed by the nurse who treated his injury. Lance had really surprised him on this trip. He was finding it harder and harder to stay mad at the boy. His resourcefulness had really impressed him and honestly, he felt a little proud. It didn't mean he wasn't going to light into him in the morning, but he really wouldn't mind hearing about the rest of his son's little adventure when he had the time.

Martin ambled down the hallway, heading towards a new section full of lights and activity that peaked his curiosity. It turned out to be the emergency room of the station's hospital. Doctors and their assistants were busy doing whatever it was that they needed to do. A limb replacement was going on in the first cubicle. Martin never ceased to be amazed at the ease in which they could now reconnect a severed arm or leg. As long as the patient didn't bleed to death on the way in, recovery was virtually one hundred percent. A lot of research funding was raised in the last century for spinal cord injuries; they too demonstrated a remarkably high recovery rate. He glanced his own injury. The thin line would barely leave a scar. The sutures would dissolve as the wound healed this way, he wouldn't have to deal with it while he was in stasis. The antibiotic treatment would be added directly to his feeding tube in order to stave off any infection. Martin was amused at the fact that he was going to go to sleep with a wound and wake up healed.

After taking a spin around the medical facility he turned to head back to the control desk. He walked up to Apollowalla at her desk, ever ready to attend to the needs of her lunar station. "Good evening, dear friend," said Martin as he greeted her. He couldn't help being excessively polite to the biosystems. He knew it wasn't like him, but he couldn't help over-romanticizing them a little bit. They were after all (as far as Martin was concerned) the guardians of space.

"Hello, Martin. I am always amazed at how easy it is for humans to forgo sleep when they need it the most." Martin grinned. Biosystems were often amused by human contradictions.

"Sometimes we need to burn off some nervous energy," Martin went on trying to explain one of the many complexities that made humans human. He also explained the situation with Joe and the two nefarious men he had befriended.

"You should be fine. I'll add additional watches to your flight," she quickly went to the control panel, typed in a few details and said, "You're all set. Your take-off is scheduled for six a.m. tomorrow. I'll see you before you leave."

"Thanks," said Martin and he headed off toward his room. Each time he went back to his berth or came from it, he tried to take a different route, so as to see as much of the massive station possible. He managed to find the biolabs where young biosystems were being developed and raised. It was a strange process and the security around the facility was extremely tight. He made sure to keep his distance.

When Martin reached the berth area and climbed into his bed again to grab a few final moments of sleep. His overhead viewing screen came on after what seemed like seconds to him. "Good morning. Mr. Mercer. Please wake up for your departure." Martin was still groggy, but sat up, just as Joe was knocking at his door.

"Rise and shine buddy!" He hollered at Martin's door.

"I'm up. I'm up!" Martin as he quickly gathered together his belongings and left with Joe. First stop was to check with Apollowalla about the biosystem she had promised to round up to watch over Lance.

"He'll be here in just a minute. Brendle was very excited to have some company for a while. He loves kids, but he was bred to help be a caregiver. Oh, there he comes now."

Martin and Joe looked up to see a short, leafy biosystem almost skipping toward them. He wore a grin much too broad for the early hour. However, an instant feeling of warmth emitted from the little green guy. "Hope I'm not late. I was talking to PoPo and he was telling me stories about his wonderful parents. I guess I lost track of time."

"You're just fine, Brendle." said Martin. "It's my son, Lance that you'll be watching. I'm happy to meet you."

"When can I see your mischievous son?" Brendle asked. He had been told about the boy's method of transport to the Station.

"Right now, if you like. He's aboard my ship."

"Brendle, you know I don't approve of your association with PoPo," Apollowalla said to Brendle. Martin was always interested in biosystem interactions with each other. He knew it was rude to listen in, but then again, the biosystems may not mind. "You are not mechanically inclined Brendle, and PoPo's personality is not one you should be emulating. Your personality is much more appropriate for your function."

"Okay, my friend. Can I go meet my new ward now?" Brendle said with a smile.

"Behave. My goodness. Sometimes you act younger than your charges!" As he left, Apollowalla looked after him smiling, "What a lovely creature he is. Simple at times, but so kind and caring and extremely efficient at his job. I know he will take good care of your son."

"I don't believe I've ever met PoPo. Is he new to the lunar station?" Martin asked.

"PoPo is new to the lunar station but was one of the first biosystems. That is part of the reason he isn't qualified for human interactions, but then again, he is bred to enjoy his solitude. He has a brilliant mind for engineering and his efforts are a large reason the lunar station has been able to achieve such a rapid amount of growth in such a short time. During the neophyte stages of biosystem development, some biosystems were derived from the hybrid genes of both humans and plants. Since then, the use of human genetic information has been banned, but the brilliant PoPo was one of the results, with massive strength, flexibility, and an amazing mind for creating and inventing. He is often described as cunning, but without conscience. I believe the word is 'sinister". He doesn't disdain human life, that likely would have ensured his destruction early in his development, but I do doubt that he holds humanity in any high value. His dedication is to maintain and improve the station and he is ideal for that."

Martin said his goodbyes to Apollowalla and with Joe in tow headed back to the ship.

* * * * *

Lance was already up, dressed and packed by the time he heard his father calling out to him from the docking bay entrance. Little did Martin know, he had been out exploring all night and now knew how he could get to SOHOIII. His father would just have to deal with it.

"I'm ready, Dad," he answered.

"Glad to see you being so cooperative, son."

"Well, if you can't beat 'em, join 'em, right Dad?"

"Uh, right, son."

Lance waved to Joe who was looking at him peculiarly. Lance didn't really know what to make of his dad's new co-pilot. He didn't seem to get annoyed at Lance, though, so he kind of liked him. He shrugged at Joe and Joe grinned back at him.

"Lance, I'd like you to meet Brendle. He's going to be your companion for the next few weeks. You can call him whenever you need to with this remote system, however, he can track you, as well," said Martin, clamping a bracelet on Lance.

"Dad! What is this?" shouted Lance.

"It's just a homing device that lets Brendle know where you are at all times and still allows you the freedom to move about the space station. This way, he can always make sure you're safe."

Lance glared at his father as Brendle stepped in. "It's really not a big deal, Lance. You have to understand that it's just a crazy policy for anyone under the age of experience level. If you look at all the kids, whose parents live here, you will see that they all have them on, too. If you like, I can get you one in a different color."

"No, prison silver will be just fine," Lance said bitterly.

"Well, then. I guess we're off," said Martin uncomfortably. He reached out to hug his son who stiffened under his embrace. "Take care. And remember, I do love you."

Lance just shrugged as he watched his father and Joe board their ship. His mind was already working on an alternative plan of escape before the shuttle ever cleared the dock.

"Want to get something to eat, Buddy?" asked Brendle.

"Um, sure. Okay." Lance didn't want to set off this guy's warning light. He'd have to play along until he came up with an idea. The two went down the hallway to the Café. They ordered a hearty breakfast and Lance wasn't shy about eating a lot. He knew he had to stock up on food if he was to survive the long trip. After breakfast. Lance excused himself, claiming he wanted to go read in the library. Brendle gave him his space, promising to check in on him whenever he remoted. Lance headed to the main library, knowing it would show up that he was indeed there. However, there were a lot of places to hide between workstations so he could work on that damn bracelet.

Lance secreted himself behind a massive row of computers in the antiquity section. He studied the mechanism for a few minutes. He chuckled. It was a simple magnetic binder. A break in the polarization would send off an alarm. However, if he could make the two magnets believe the pull was still there, he could slip it off, no problem. All he needed was a thin magnet. "Where could he get one?" The medical center! They used magnets everywhere in the surgery unit. He'd pull one off of a laser mount. The only trick would be to get in and out without getting caught. Lance had the answer. He pushed the remote. He'd just walk right in, with Brendle at his side.

In just a matter of seconds, the bio-nanny was at his side. Somewhat winded, he asked, "What's up? Did you need something?"

"Oh," said Lance, doubling over. "I think that tofu I had for breakfast got to me."

"Oh dear," bemoaned Brendle. "Let's get you to bed."

"No, I think it's food poisoning." Lance said, making himself gag.

"I haven't heard of a case of that for nearly ten years. It must be something else," the little creature said.

"Well, whatever it is, it's bad." moaned Lance.

"Let's go to the medical center. Can you walk?"

"I'll try," said Lance weakly. The two made their way slowly to the doctors' station.

"You wait right here. I'll get a nurse," said Brendle. He'd never had this happen before. An occasional cut or bruise, yes, but not an all-out illness. He quickly found a triage biosystem and headed her over to his ward. "See what's wrong with him, please," implored Brendle.

The biosystem took Lance's vitals with a body scanner. "Hmm everything is reading normal. Let's get him on a table and I'll send a doctor in."

That was the break Lance was looking for. He knew he'd be asked to disrobe, and they would certainly give him privacy for that. Sure enough, that's exactly what happened. The moment he was alone, Lance grabbed a magnet plate off of a laser scan in the room and shoved it far down into his pants pocket. Just as the doctor entered, he forced out his loudest and most obnoxious belch.

"Whew! Do I feel better! Must have been some major gas there, doc. Sorry to have troubled you." Lance hopped off the table, quickly dressed and gave the doctor a sheepish grin. "Guess I ought to lay off those mineral seltzers, huh?"

Brendle was wringing his limbs as Lance emerged. "Nothing to worry about, old shrub. Just some normal bodily emissions!"

The bio-nanny was hesitant to leave Lance, but the boy insisted he was just fine, and he promised to summon him should he take a turn for the worse. Grudgingly, Brendle left and went back to the card game he had been playing.

Lance wasted no time removing the bracelet and hooking it onto a lower leg of a maid's cart. That way it would keep moving around and he could go on with his business.

The boy scurried to the loading docks. The night before, he had come upon an old transport pod; one used for simple commuter trips to and from the nearest planets. It looked antiquated outside, however, once Lance had gotten inside of it, he marveled at the technology. Someone had been rebuilding this pod. All of the systems worked beautifully, some were more advanced than anything he had ever seen. It hadn't taken him long to figure them out or so he thought, and now he was putting his escape plan into action. He couldn't help but wonder whose incredible ship this was and why he was developing it. He had found a map of Venus and its orbital schedule on board. Odd, he thought because the colonization of that planet had been discontinued. Funding had stopped years ago, and now it contained only a shell of a space center that was mostly underground. Yet the map looked strangely new.

As he looked around more, he came upon some research notes. "The Micro-biosystems" was the title of one set. He had heard of some research being done in this field but was unaware that it was actually being accomplished. A rather notorious scientist had come up with an idea for creating little biosystems.

He had managed to snag some food supplies from his father's ship as well as the snack bar near the central desk. He was ready for takeoff. He plugged into the main computer to make certain no one else would be in the airspace at that same time. He found the atmosphere to be uncontested. Lance cleared himself for takeoff.

The pod shuttered and then broke free, shooting itself into outer space. Lance programmed in the coordinates for SOHOIII. The sophisticated aircraft he had pirated could fly itself all the way: dodging meteors and any other space debris it might encounter.

Lance settled in for stasis. He set the wake-up program for three days outside of SOHOIII. He'd show his dad a thing or two.

In the meantime, Martin and Joe had a successful liftoff. There appeared to be no one following them, and once the craft was stable, Martin got on the telecommute to talk to Nicole. She answered right away.

"How are you, darling?" he asked.

"Missing you, of course." Nicole answered. He had wakened her, but that didn't matter. She loved to hear from him whenever she could.

"I got Lance squared away with a great bio-nanny on the Lunar Station."

"That's nice. I still wish you had taken him, but I don't want to rehash an old argument." she said.

"I promise to spend more time with him when we get home.""

"I'm going to hold you to that." Nicole said.

"Well, get back to sleep, angel."

"Talk to me soon, Marty."

His next call was to Bill Harding's home. Apollowalla had alerted the Solar Scanners. They were the twenty-first century's answer to the Highway Patrol, just faster ships, who were on the lookout for the Kitty Hawk.

The telecommute finally got through. Bill's brother, Stanley was there. "I don't mean to intrude but is Bill all right?" asked Martin.

"Are you a friend?" asked the brother.

"Yes, a very good friend. I went to school with Bill. If you look on his fireplace mantel, there's a picture of the two of us."

Stanley did just that. Sure enough, on the mantel was a picture of a much younger Martin with his helmet between his legs and his arm around Bill's neck in a playful pose.

"I guess you haven't heard. Bill's in the hospital. Got a concussion, but he's going to be okay. Some bastard stole his ship. Came in, conked my brother on the head and stole his identifier bar. With that, it didn't take the culprit anytime at all to zoom off in Bill's little pride and joy. I'm just thankful my brother's okay."

"My God," said Marty. "I have to tell you the reason I called, however. I saw the Kitty Hawk."

"Where?" asked Stanley excitedly.

"At the docking bay on the Lunar Station. I just left. We reported it and there's a posse out after the thieves now, that's the best we could do."

"That's encouraging. Would you please keep me posted? I'll be staying with Bill until he's better."

"No problem, but you might have better luck checking with the Solar Scanners themselves," answered Martin.

"I'll do that, and thanks again."

They signed off and Martin turned to Joe who was piloting the rig. "I'm going to confirm with SOHOIII that we are on course and will be there soon before I go into stasis."

Martin called up the main computer at the isolated space station. His old friend. Gila answered.

"How are you, Marty?" he asked.

"Just fine, friend. We're on our way. Should see you very soon. We've got those supplies you ordered, too."

"Excellent! Umm, by the way, I'm going to need a favor."

"What's that?" asked Martin.

"There's a stranded passenger here. Her ship was stolen right out from under our nose. Don't know how it happened and she is really angry. Her name's Yvette. She's a Russian national. Tiny little thing, but a temper out of this world."

"We'll do what we can, but we're pretty crowded in here. If she doesn't mind sharing space, we'll accommodate her. Wow, I can't believe thieves have resorted to stealing whole ships now and not just the collectors anymore. I've seen a few suspicious activities already this trip and now you tell me a ship was stolen right under your nose. Something is going on Gila so we must really be on our toes. I'll talk to you again once we reach Venus. I find it is too hard on this aging body to sleep the whole way. It makes my recovery quicker if I awaken halfway through the journey." explained Martin excitedly still gasping from the news of a ship stolen from SOHOIII.

"It's settled then. I'll tell her she has a ride home. That should make my next few weeks a bit more pleasant. I'll keep my eyes and computer open as well, Marty. If I hear anything I'll let you know and as always I look forward to your visit."

Martin shut down the telecommute and contemplated checking on Lance. "Nah," he decided, "the boy is probably having a great time. I'd better just leave well enough alone. After all my years of solo running and now I'm taking on another passenger I must be crazy! Look at how much trouble I've already accumulated for myself." Martin began to question his judgment in bringing along another person and now, as fate would have it, he was thinking about adding another. This will be one run for the books.

Marty and Joe in one ship. Lance in another, all closed their eyes and settled in for the long stasis on their voyage to SOHOIII.

CHAPTER 6

VOYAGE TO SOHOIII

Meanwhile, back on the Lunar Station. Brendle was frantic. He had lost his charge. What a horrible mistake he'd made, giving the boy so much freedom. But he seemed so able, and while Brendle would certainly have loved spending the time with the lad, he also didn't want to smother him; he knew about human teenagers!

"Oh my, what am I going to do?" he moaned to himself. He thought back to the instant when he had discovered the boy had tricked him. Brendle had prepared dinner for Lance and had discovered him missing. When he had followed Lance's tracker beacon, it had led him on a merry chase across several levels of the guest berths for visiting scientists and their families. Finally, when the flashing on his optical computer indicated that the boy should be just a few feet away, Brendle had discovered a cleaning robot that was pushing a supply cart with Lance's tracker clamped sturdily around the leg. Piecing together what had happened. Brendle took off for Apollowalla's desk. His apprehension was building at the thought of telling the big biosystem what had happened, but he had no choice. He had messed up and all he could do now was face the music.

"Brendle, explain to me again what has happened. I am not sure I heard you correctly," Apollowalla was generally used to being surprised by the goings-on of humans. She often found her fellow biosystems significantly more predictable.

"I seem to have lost the boy, Walla."

"I assume he was able to find a way to remove his tracker then. How unexpected. I will be able to postpone ships disembarking for an hour or two while an investigation is conducted to identify the boy's current whereabouts," Apollowalla's efficiency was often mesmerizing to witness. Her movements were elegant as she worked the consoles around her. Quickly pulling up ship schedules and notifying the necessary parties about the boy's disappearance. "There are two potential ship launches that may have had the boy on board if he cannot be found on the station. I believe we may safely eliminate the first option since it is unlikely that Lance Mercer, at such a young age, has declared himself a delinquent in order to help pirate the Kitty Hawk. The second one, however, was an emergency pod that's been out of service for many weeks. It appears to be one of the original models, but it looks like the pilot was able to bypass the emergency systems. The pod's launch did not trigger the usual alarms." Hands continued to fly over the console, her eyes darting around as she quickly took in information and processed it with incredible speed. "The pod's destination was altered." She Apollowalla's stopped for a moment looking up at Brendle, "It is heading for SOHOIII."

Both biosystems looked up as a third biosystem appeared in the doorway of Apollowalla's office. PoPo generally liked his space. Even with his small and spindly stature, he did not step far into the office.

"Thank you for coming here directly, PoPo." said Apollowalla. "I am hoping you can give us more information on this pod in particular." Apollowalla indicated that she had just sent the information to PoPo's optical computer. "It launched not even an hour ago on its way for SOHOIII."

As one of the original biosystems, PoPo did not undergo the initial developmental conditioning that allowed him to express human emotion. Perhaps that is why his demeanor generally intimidated most humans. They had no real way to identify PoPo's thoughts, making him alien even among those that are already alien. "Apollowalla, the pod is approximately twenty years old. It was in a non-functional state but was apparently still capable of launching into space. Its original destination was intended to be Earth and for that reason, it was outfitted with the necessary shielding for re-entry into Earth's atmosphere."

"Yes, PoPo. I see that in the pod's history. Let me be more specific. Do you believe that the pod in question can be successfully piloted to SOHOIII by a fourteen-year-old human boy?"

PoPo's head cocked to the side as he processed the question. "Yes. However, the pod was in the middle of a redesign. The pod will not be capable of a return trip."

Apollowalla was able to release a sigh of relief. "This is good news. Thank you PoPo." Despite Apollowalla's dismissal, PoPo remained in the office. His expressionless face staring at Apollowalla until she looked up, "Do you intend to retrieve the pod personally then, PoPo?"

"Yes, I will take the necessary equipment to conduct the remainder of the upgrades to the pod. I will need to take shuttle number 47. It has recently been serviced and is still designated as an inactive unit."

Apollowalla looked over the schedule and nodded her agreement.

Without any further discussion Popo turned and left the office.

"I'm really sorry about this Walla. I can't begin to tell you how bad I feel," said Brendle, whose leaves were starting to wilt from stress and worry, as well as a lack of water.

"I know you didn't mean to let it happen. I believe it is a common occurrence for humans to underestimate their young. I feel you can grow from this experience Brindle, and I hope you have learned to watch your future wards more carefully. They don't even have to know you're watching," she said. "Now, go get some sleep in the photosynthesis chamber and soak up some water for a while. All will be well."

* * * * *

PoPo had lost no time making his way directly to the shuttle bay. He had already packed; in fact, he had been packed for quite some time. The circumstances might have changed, but he had been anticipating taking off from the Lunar Station in a different pod.

And now a human child had stolen that pod right out from under him. He could hear Apollowalla's voice in his head correcting his thought process. "Think of human children like your ships and how you protect and care for them, PoPo." The analogy was absurd really. The building of ships requires a powerful mind and a greater understanding of the workings of space. Raising children requires what? Proper sound dampening and waste disposal systems. He had seen a diaper once. Human children were loathsome.

It had only been a day, but Lance's stasis chamber was undergoing the wake-up processes. What? How was this possible? He checked his watch; sure enough, it had only been one Earth Day. He needed to check his course. Lance continued to fight his sleep inertia as he stumbled over to the pod's control console. He rubbed his eyes as he assessed the ship's systems. Everything looked normal... except the speed. This could not be possible. The pod should not be able to travel at these speeds. He had used the ship's recommended calculations for the journey, but the pod was traveling nearly ten times faster than he would have expected. It would take his dad and Joe over a month to reach SOHOIII. He would accomplish it in days.

THUD! Lance was nearly thrown to the floor, barely catching himself on the console. Did something just hit the pod?! THUD! He was slammed forward. He gathered his thoughts and looked outside. Some sort of space debris was impacting the ship. Frantically, he surveyed the panel of controls. He pushed a button labeled "shield" and hoped for the best. A slight whirring noise was all he heard as he watched a thin wall of metal encase his pod. From that point on, tiny taps, almost like an earthly hailstorm, were all he heard. Lance smiled to himself. His dad always made piloting sound so complex. Maybe it was just this ship, but so far everything had seemed fairly intuitive. "Or maybe it's just easy for genius boy pilot Lance Mercer! Bring it on space!" He was feeling quite pleased with himself as he plopped down into the pilot's chair propping his feet up on the console. He eyed the large display centrally located in the console and started tabbing through display options, "I bet this thing has some video games."

When the tapping outside subsided and Lance was bored of his fruitless hunt for entertainment, he decided to take down the shield. His view of space returned and sure enough, there it was, Venus. "Venus doesn't listen well. Forgets what other planets tell. The second planet from the sun spins the other way for fun..." Lance recited a poem his third-grade teacher had taught them and grinned at the deadly planet. "You and me both Venus."

Something caught his eye and he squinted into space moving closer to the viewing panel. He knew the big planet was supposed to be deserted; the plans for a station there had been halted... There it was again! Something else was out there, should he take a look? What if it was space pirates? He could report that to his father and be a hero! At the speed this pod could travel, one look and he could hightail it out of there. He knew taking the pod off course and flying manually would be no easy task for a beginner, but his curiosity was peaked.

Shutting down autopilot, he slowed the ship and guided it towards Venus. By following the indicators on the console, he was careful to stay out of the planet's gravitational pull. "This is way too easy." The moving object had left his field of vision but as he approached, the telltale sign of light flashing off of metal caught his eye. Sure enough, hovering all around one particular area, were several ships.

Like most imprudent teenagers, Lance was adept at ignoring the warning alarms going off in his own head. The ship's warning alarms though, were much more difficult to ignore. Like the space debris, the shot came from out of the blue... or black as it were. Ping! It resounded off the pod. Lance dove for the shield button again. He managed to close it up just as he was pelted with a barrage of shots. The ships were actually shooting at him! He knew almost nothing about this pod. What if the shielding didn't hold?

He had seen the "cloaking" button earlier. Once he reached SOHOIII testing that particular button had been topping his to-do list, but now without any hesitation, Lance slammed his hand down on it. The shots didn't stop. His only chance was escape. If he let the ships close, they may have the capability to grapple and reign in his little pod or worse. They could pull out the close-range high powered weaponry and just obliterate him and pick up the pieces. "I just need a second to think. How do I turn off these stupid alarms?" With that thought, something large struck the pod on the port side. Panicked Lance tripped over the pilot's chair, his chin struck the console on his way down. He curled up into a ball on the floor clutching his hurting head and tasting blood as he tried to stop the spinning. Additional alarms began to go off indicating that the shielding had been pierced and the pod jerked.

"NO!" With shaking hands Lance pulled himself up into the pilot's chair. The only plan he had was Plan A: high tail it out of there. He altered his course, aiming away from Venus and its host of dangerous space bandits, and gunned it. The pod jerked forward but was being held in place. He increased his throttle and covered his ears as the sounds of metal tearing pervaded the pod's interior. Lance gripped his head with tears and blood streaming down his face, trying to squeeze the reality that he was about to die out of his own mind. All he wanted in that one brief moment as the consequences of all of his rash decisions collapsed down on him was his father.... was the man who tried so very hard to keep Lance out of situations like these. With one final metallic scream, the pod shot forward. The chorus of shots began to taper off and finally stopped.

It took another ten minutes before Lance moved. The ship's alarms were still flashing and blaring. Lance's heart continued to pound, but his mind had begun to work again as it tried to sort through the confusion that he was still alive...still alive and gaining distance from deadly, deadly Venus.

* * * * *

Martin awoke from his stasis as scheduled in order to run basic status updates on the ship. He stumbled to the toilet fighting against the nausea that always came after extended amounts of time in stasis and eventually lost, like he always did. Picking himself up, he started running the ship's status checks. He was about halfway through when he saw that they had received a communications signal. It was about a week old from Apollowalla updating him on what was going on with his son. His anger soon gave way to fear as the magnitude of the danger his son was in hit him. Apollowalla had informed him about PoPo's pursuit, and the thought did little to comfort him. There was something inherently off about that biosystem. He made the decision to not wake Joe. Martin used the time alone to vent his frustrations with some body weight exercises and then afterwards he took one of the few "showers" he would be afforded on the trip to SOHOIII. The shower was really just enough to wet his hair twice, once for soaping and once for rinsing and towel off the rest of him. He felt a little better, but Martin was never a patient man. Every fiber of his body wanted to act; to go find his son and get him home. He knew that trying to make the trip without stasis could be dangerous, but what if he missed further communication.

He remembered a story about a couple of "cowboys" who decided they could make the trip without stasis. They had stayed awake for many days before, so what was a few more? And besides, they could take their regular naps. Space flight, however, has a much different effect on the body than under regular conditions. Without stasis, the body atrophies much faster and the brain can become under stimulated or confused. The investigators believe that only a few days had passed before both men went crazy. The stronger of the two murdered the other in what appeared to be a very violent manner. When the ship arrived at the station, a confused and agitated man collapsed at the feet of those who came to greet the shuttle. No one that he had heard of had tried making the trip without stasis since.

A thousand scenarios were flooding Martin's mind. Could he find his son? He was theoretically on the same or a similar course as Martin currently, if Apollowalla's information was correct. He should be behind him. It would be dangerous to wait, Martin knew that. If he did by some miracles happen across his son what then? Strap on space suits, open up and pull him aboard? Not unheard of, but that was also dangerous. He would need Joe to pilot the other ship back. It may work, but the odds were not in their favor. Martin shook his head; none of these options were in any way practical. The success rate was just too low. He decided he had no choice but to go into stasis and continue on his current course.

The gears in his head were grinding as he doubled the number of times he would be broken out of stasis. He typed up a note to Joe updating him, since he was due to be woken up next. Before climbing into his stasis pod, he made sure Joe's vitals were all standard and let his thoughts wander as he tried to relax before entering stasis. Joe was going to be a great pilot. He seemed easy-going enough, with a good head on his shoulders. Martin never tried to press Joe about his past recognizing that it was a topic Joe tried to avoid. "Sometimes, the past is better left to journals of the mind." Martin grinned at his philosophical thought as he climbed into his stasis pod. Then, once again. Martin closed his eyes and drifted into weightlessness.

* * * * *

Lance couldn't believe it! In just a matter of minutes, he would be landing on SOHOIII. This was really a dream come true for him. He had heard of this place for the last three years, from his father and from school. He had researched it on his computer and even gone there taking a virtual tour. He had so many questions. He just hoped that he wouldn't be stuck somewhere in a cage for "escaping".

After his encounter with the space pirates the pod had been in bad shape. Even after he managed to turn the hull integrity alarms off they kept coming back on. He knew the inner hull hadn't been breached, but the outer shielding would not retract. The ship itself was traveling much slower than it had originally and he had needed to bypass three different status checks to get the ship back into autopilot at all. All in all, it set him back several days. He had jumped back into stasis, but the ship systems kept waking him up again whenever the alarms would trigger, so he was stuck awake, dealing with phantom alarms and with nothing else to do. Approaching SOHOIII was a miracle, but at the same time the gravity of what he had done was nearly paralyzing in scope. He realized he had stolen a spacecraft, damaged it and broken several universal space laws. They wouldn't send a fourteen-year-old to prison would they?

As far as he knew, though, there was no law enforcement on SOHOIII. It was primarily inhabited by a single individual; another biosystem by the name of Gila. He knew little of this particular scientist, only that he had been selected from thousands of applicants for the position; a coveted one in the science world. He also knew that his father thought very highly of him. Hopefully, Gila would understand.

Lance saw SOHOIII approaching in his scanner window. He prepared for landing and was only mildly surprised at the smooth way the pod glided itself onto a waiting runway, and into a docking bay. As soon as he was given the all-clear, he began to pass through the series of airlocks that laboriously goes through each layer of shielding around the station. Finally, and apprehensively, he took a step out of the last airlock where he came face to face with a middle-aged, bespectacled biosystem. "I'm going to take a wild guess here, and ask if your name is Lance Mercer, by any chance?" he asked the boy.

"Oh, you've heard of me, huh?" he answered.

"Oh, my yes. You're in a lot of trouble, young man," said Gila.

"I know. I know, but I just had to come. I've been dreaming about your work here forever. I know so much about this place and I figured I'd never get another chance to experience it, otherwise," said Lance.

Gila softened a bit. "Well, I must admit, I've been impressed by you as well. You made it here in one piece. That's quite an accomplishment. You've lucked out, however. No one wants to press charges against you for anything yet. However, if I know your dad, and I do, I wouldn't be expecting to have much of a social life for the next, oh forty years if I were you!"

"I'll cross that bridge when I come to it," answered Lance trying to imitate one of his father's favorite sayings.

"So, is this the famous, boy wonder?" asked a heavily accented female voice.

"Oh, Lance, this is Yvette Karrnoff. She has been my guest since her ship was stolen right out from under her, here at SOHOIII. She will be returning to Earth aboard your father's ship."

Lance felt the breath get sucked right out of him. He hadn't really heard anything Gila had said. All he could do was gaze at the beautiful woman before him. Yvette stood only five feet tall, a few inches shorter than even young Lance, but oh! What they had packed into those five feet! Her light brown hair fell long and softly around her face. Her skin was tanned and smooth, her eyes large and green. Perfect, white teeth shone through very full lips, just below a tiny, turned-up nose. Lance had no clue that women could look like this. All he ever saw were his mother and sister. At school, girls were just a part of the background. He didn't have many girls who were friends and he had exactly zero girlfriends.

It didn't matter that she was, at least, ten years older than he was: all he knew was that he was in love!

Lance knew he was staring. Staring was supposed to be bad... wasn't it? He really should stop now... shouldn't he? Gila broke the awkward scene placing his hand-like-appendage on Lance's shoulder. "I think it is very important that we contact the Lunar Station right now. Lance. You seem to be... tired... no? I am sorry. This expression you are making is difficult for me to read."

Lance looked at Gila taking a second to process his words followed by instant mortification. He felt his face flush completely and suddenly found the ground extremely interesting. "Oh...rig... right," his voice cracked deepening his blush. He was pretty sure his face was about to melt off.

"Aww, now you are embarrassed. That one I recognize. Come along, we have already primed the comms. It should only take a moment to connect to the Lunar station." Gila guided him into what must be the communications hub for the station. It was pretty small and didn't quite fit the three of them, but Lance imagined everything in SOHOIII was economically built. His hand brushed Yvette's and he pulled it away as if she had burned him. Oh man... How uncool was that? He should have left it there, anyone cool would have left it there! Maybe he should put it back. Lance was distracted trying to figure out how to put his hand back down without looking too obvious.

"SOHOIII to the Lunar Station. Our connection seems to be unstable. Apollowalla are you there?" Gila's voice broke into his daydream.

Apollowalla's alien visage appeared on the screen, her voice once again making Lance flinch. "Hello Gila. The connection is not strong, but I see and hear you." Apollowalla's image seemed to freeze as they dealt with a delay in the communications. Then her eyes flicked to Lance. "Oh fantastic! The wayward Lance Mercer has been found. Are you of able body and mind, child?"

Lance flinched again. Did she have to call him a child? Yvette might not know how old he is. "Hi, Apollowalla. Ya, I'm ok. I uhh... the ship it...I really did not mean to damage it Apollowalla."

Yvette snorted a laugh behind him, "Walla, from a cursory glance, he's somehow managed to destroy around forty percent of the outer shielding. It also looked like the propulsion engines were suffering. Given the speeds he was traveling at, I would say they were overclocked and on the verge of overheating. I didn't recognize some of the systems on this pod, though. It's incredible. Is it a new design?" Yvette's accent, was it Russian? Was like music to Lance.

"I believe it is a re-design that PoPo has been working on. His reports had not indicated anything of this magnitude, though. It is not unlike PoPo to under embellish, though. I am glad all is well with you Lance Mercer. You truly did make excellent time. I will pass the word on to your father. Gila, I will require that you disable the ship, so we do not lose the boy again?" Lance flinched for a third time. Ok, maybe he did deserve that.

"I'm sure we will think of a way to keep Lance Mercer station bound. If out thinking this child has provided you a challenge, Apollowalla, then I am ever so excited to rise to the occasion as it were." Gila started making an awful gasping noise. Lance was confused until he realized it was Gila's attempt at laughter.

"You males and your competitive natures. Goodbye Gila, Miss Karrnoff, and Lance Mercer." She sighed and signed off.

Lance was a little surprised. He understood that emotions were not really the forte of the Biosystems, but no one even seemed angry. For now, he would count his blessings because when his dad arrived, he knew all of that would change. Gila turned to Yvette. "Will you show Lance to his bunk? I will work on disabling the pod. Maybe I should just de-pressurize the docking bay. It might upset PoPo less if I actually locked down the ships systems. Yes, I think that will be a good start. Even if you bypass the pressurization systems for the docking bay, young Lance Mercer, it will take time before you will be able to pass through."

"Uhh...well ok Gila, but you really don't need to. I don't want leave SOHOIII." replied Lance.

Gila began his awful gasping wheeze again, "Yes, well your subterfuge will not work on me."

Yvette rolled her eyes and tapped Lance on the shoulder, "Come along little flyboy." she teased.

They could hear Gila mutter as they began to walk down the corridor. "If he uses a space suit, though... he'll be able to get through. Hmm... What if I increased the gravity?"

Lance shared a glance with Yvette as she laughed at Gila's musing. He didn't know where they were heading, but he would have followed her anywhere! She led him into a small building that was attached to the hangers. There were only about twenty bunking chambers; so very small compared to the mammoth space station he had just left. They walked down to the third door, and Yvette said, "I am sure you will be sleeping soundly very soon. Your eyelids look leaden. Goodnight!"

She left and headed back down the hallway to where Gila was. Lance sighed, pulled up a picture of Yvette in his mind and fell promptly asleep with a huge grin on his face.

Martin sat up with a jolt. The scheduling for his stasis routine was bizarre to his body. He was used to being under longer and he was not adapting well. It took him a minute to clear his head, fighting nausea once again.

Once he had adjusted, he checked immediately for word about Lance and sure enough, they had received a communication.

"Hello, again Martin." Apollowalla's voice came through, it was hard to tell but did she seem happy? "I am pleased to inform you that your son, Lance Mercer has arrived at SOHOIII."

What? Thought Martin. There was no way Lance was already there.

"The pod your son had...mmm...confiscated was newly designed by PoPo himself. It apparently has capabilities that outclass most normal spacecraft. I have directed Gila to ensure that Lance Mercer does not leave SOHOIII. They are awaiting your arrival. I hope the remainder of your trip is safe and routine. Apollowalla out."

Martin sat for a moment and gathered his thoughts. How in the world did that pod make it there so fast? He would have to see it when he reached SOHOIII. His relief was so intense that Martin's hands were shaking. He laughed at himself as he adjusted his stasis alarm to wake him at Venus, the halfway point. Generally, he liked to break up the lengthy sleep on the journey; that made the recovery quicker. While stasis kept a man sane, coming out of too long of a stasis could be excruciating. He remembered his first time. The headache was so bad all he could do was sit with his hands pressing on the sides of his temples for two days, vomiting and cramping all the while. Nicole had joked that at least now he could appreciate PMS; for which there still wasn't a cure! However, he found that if he woke himself up at least once, the effects were very minimal. With that, he slipped back into stasis.

Lance slept for nearly two days; when he awoke his body was stiff from the sleep, but his mind was running at warp speed. He then became Gila's shadow and the biosystem seemed to really enjoy the company. Gila took him to his greenhouse. It was the biosystem's pride and joy. The greenhouse area was easily the largest chamber in the entire station and equipped with a state-of-the-art laboratory. There was even a bed in the corner of the lab where Gila said he spent many nights in order to be close to his work. The lab was well equipped, and it took incredible efforts to keep it up to date since the station was so out of the way. Gila showed Lance his hybrid collections and all his research on soil types. Lance was enthralled and for a moment was completely mesmerized by what he was seeing. This was his dream and now he knew that it was also his future. He knew that he would be spending his life doing just what Gila was doing.

Every day they would run into Yvette. Gila chuckled to himself, watching the bright youngster go stupid at the sight of her. "I do believe that your pairing would be unlikely, Lance," said Gila one day.

"What are you talking about?" said Lance, turning bright red.

"I am sorry to say that the hormones you are producing at the site of Miss Yvette are only one sided."

"Well, you have to admit, she's pretty," answered Lance. "Yes, well, if you like that type. All skin, no roots."

"Oh, but look at those stems!" laughed Lance.

"They'd look better in green." retorted Gila. The biosystem looked at Lance fondly. He had been surprised by the harmonious relationship developing between himself and the young human. Not for the first time, Gila suspected that the boy would make an ideal protégé. His studies were his life, and there were few individuals that he would ever trust with such an accumulation of knowledge. His judgment of Lance was that he was just the one for that job. He could tell by the sparkle in his eyes and by the quality of the questions asked by the boy.

Lance continued to marvel at how well equipped the laboratory was as Gila described his research. "To work with genetic combinations requires some very technical equipment. I've developed two new species of plants with advanced photosynthesis which has many growers very excited. The improved energy production may help to achieve significant advances in biosystem development."

The research mesmerized Lance. This is what he had always dreamed of doing, creating new life and finding cures to old problems. He knew that someday; he would be doing just that.

* * * * *

As planned, Martin awoke from stasis when they reached Venus. He was shaking off the effects of stasis and enjoying a good long look at Lady Venus when a ship suddenly appeared in his viewer. "Hello, what have we here?" He watched the ship speed toward Venus. Had that ship seen them? He ran to the pilot's console, dropping the ship out of autopilot. He needed to adjust their course. They would lose about a day, but if there were strange ships out here, he did not want to go anywhere near that planet. Using the communicator this close to strange activity could be dangerous. The one problem with space communications was that they were so easy to intercept for anyone who was looking for them. He didn't want his inquiries to be overheard by whoever was out there, just in case it wasn't on the up and up. Martin checked all of Joe's readings and determined that he was fine. He made some coffee and sat down to begin sentry duty until they were farther away from Venus. Finally, he decided he was ready to secure himself for the final leg of the journey. Two weeks to SOHOIII. He uttered a wish to the stars that this last part would be uneventful. There had been way too many incidences already!

CHAPTER 7

TO CATCH A FLARE

When Joe slipped deeply into stasis the dreams began. They were not really nightmares because they didn't frighten him. They just filled him with a sort of melancholy. He could vaguely make out his mother's face beautiful and soft. He always remembered her as fair, and she seemed so fragile. He didn't start thinking of her as young until lately, but as he got older, he began to recognize her as such. She was kissing him on the cheek and a tear was streaming down her face. "I love you, little Joey. Don't you ever forget that."

In the dreams he had forgotten why his mom was so unhappy. And the realization that he was being taken from her was new and painful then his mom was gone. No familiar faces, just a big house with lots of children. Two older ladies took care of him. They were nice enough and very strict with his schooling, but there were so many other kids there, he never got much attention. Joe could slip into his own world, where he could escape during the bad times or lonely hours. In his mind he was flying; big ships and aircraft filled his every thought. The aircraft would morph into spacecraft and everything in between, but they always represented a feeling of freedom. From the age of six, all he ever wanted to be a pilot, the best in the world.

* * * * *

Joe awakened with the most awful headache he had ever had. "Ugg... just please shoot me now."

Martin chuckled, "I guess I should have warned you about "bed head.""

"What the hell is that?" moaned Joe.

"That's what you get from full stasis. I know, it sucks, but every pilot has to go through it once. I'll tell you how to avoid it next time."

"Bastard," muttered Joe, as he painfully stepped out of his bunk. Martin had to marvel, however, at how quickly Joe seemed to recover. Ah, the benefits of youth.

"You ready to land this thing?" asked Martin after Joe began to look better.

"Yeah, I think so," answered Joe. Once again, the young pilot made a perfect landing. Martin knew that Joe was going to be one of the best. He was already as good at landings as most experienced pilots were, including himself. The craft slowly pulled into its assigned hanger and the two men waited patiently for all the systems to shut down. They raised the door and stepped out into the world of SOHOIII.

"A bit small, isn't it?" remarked Joe.

"Sure, but it's state-of-the-art. Even the Lunar Station doesn't have some of the toys that Gila gets to play with. Be careful disembarking through the series of chambers. There will be a three-minute wait in each before moving on to the next. This protects the sterile environment that Gila needs for his research as well as allowing us passage through the many layers of shielding protecting SOHOIII. We probably need to secure the ship, since apparently one was just stolen from here."

"Wait, what? Someone stole a ship way out here?" Joe exclaimed as a huge banging sound filled the room.

"That was the protective radiation shield closing in our ship. Can't be too careful!" answered Martin. The two men grabbed a nearby forklift and loaded up the supplies they were carrying for Gila. Navigating around the small areas with the forklift was challenging. It required that the forklift be turned in place, which it was capable of, but was a slow and tedious process. Finally, they entered the first of the chambers allowing them access to the station. The chambers were very small, barely large enough for the cargo and the two men. Martin and Joe would have to wait pressed between the sides of the cargo and the interior walls of the chamber. This was really the one part of SOHOIII that Martin actually hated. After being in a tiny ship for weeks the thought of being able to walk around in the larger chambers of the space stations was sometimes almost overwhelming. Then to be denied that at the end of the journey and instead crammed into these tiny chambers for twenty minutes was borderline maddening. Martin heard a stream of cursing coming from the other side of the forklift. "You ok over there Joe?"

"Pinched my damn hand. I can barely breathe over here Martin. How much room you got?" asked Joe.

"The same as you, hang in there, only about four more chambers left."

"Easy for you to say, my head is killing me. No time like the present to start becoming claustrophobic." Martin chuckled but did not disagree. Martin's sigh of relief was dwarfed by Joe's when they finally reached the landing bay where Gila, Yvette, and Lance were awaiting their arrival.

"Welcome aboard, my dear friend!" greeted Gila, shaking Martin's hand.

"Hello, Gila. You look great." he replied. "This is my co-pilot, Joe." The two greeted each other, as Martin looked over to Lance. The boy had positioned himself as far away from his father as the chamber allowed. His shoulders and head were slumped over in a true hangdog expression and if his eyes happened to meet his father's they would instantly drop back down to the floor. Martin walked over to Lance and pulled him into a giant bear hug. "You ever do something this stupid again, and you'll need a telescope to see freedom." He said in his son's ear. All Lance could do was hug his dad back, nod fervently and make garbled attempts at choking out an apology. "Have you contacted your mother?"

"Ya..." Lance said with more nodding. Martin stepped back letting the boy wipe his eyes.

"Martin, Joe, this is Yvette," Gila said giving Lance a minute to compose himself.

"Very pleased to meet you." said Joe, taking Yvette's hand gently. She quickly pulled it back and said to him, "I don't like to be touched."

Joe, only slightly rebuffed said, "Maybe on our second date."

"I wouldn't count on it," she huffed. "Pleased to meet you, Martin. I appreciate the ride to Earth." With that, she turned and left the room.

"Now that's the most impressive sight I've seen on this station yet," said Joe.

Gila disagreed by performing his rendition of a human snort, "That one has been intolerable since her ship was stolen. I'll never understand humans' inability to direct their tempers properly."

"Sounds like she just needs an outlet." laughed Joe. Martin shook his head. He had heard that Joe was a bit of a ladies' man, but somehow, he didn't seem all that concerned about Yvette.

Gila frowned, "We may not be as large as the Lunar Station here on SOHOIII, but I assure you that we have plenty of outlets. I even have a dozen different adapters and buck booster transformers if those are what she needs."

Joe grinned at Gila, "Something tells me that even an impressive station like SOHOIII isn't going to have the necessary tools she needs." Lance started to cough; his face had turned a shade of red that was bordering on purple. Joe had walked over to Lance clapping him on the back to "help" him through his coughing fit, "Hey Lance! Enjoying space?"

Lance perked up at the younger pilot rubbing his newly bruised shoulder, "Hi Joe! Ya, it's great."

Gila, shaking his head as he wrote Joe's comment off as a human-just-being-human, turned to the forklift full of cargo. "Excellent, I see my supplies have arrived... Oooh is that my Cactus and Succulent Society order?" Gila started rummaging through the crates as Lance stepped up behind him to help him stack things on the floor around the chamber. "Everything looks to be in good shape. I sure appreciate the delivery." Martin watched the biosystem and his son working together. Lance still wasn't looking Martin in the eye, but his son seemed to be quite comfortable around Gila as they rapidly continued opening boxes with Gila muttering as he checked off items from a mental list.

"Gila, how did they steal a docked ship from SOHOIII? They would have had to get past all the shielding gates," asked Martin.

"From what we can tell, they sent an internal signal from the ship itself essentially requesting dock release but bypassing all the main security checks. The shields opened and they came in and took the ship." Gila closed up one of the crates he had been sorting through and came over to stand next to Martin. "We've been in contact with the Lunar Station and they're sending down an investigation team, but it will be a while before they get here. For now, we've had to keep the system on manual. The shields will only respond to a direct input of my personal code and physically flipping the release switch in the command chamber. It's basic I know, but if our system is compromised then taking it off of automation is really the only fix. It makes things a little more complicated for my experimentation, but I have been assured that it is in everyone's best interest that we keep the station as locked down as possible."

"Damn, a signal from inside the station? I didn't even think that was possible unless the pirates had help from someone in the station."

"That is very unlikely, Martin. I do not believe Yvette helped them steal her own ship and I have never seen the scientific value in space piracy."

Martin looked up as Joe sidled over, "Hey Martin, mind showing me where the bunks are?"

"Ya sure, Joe. Gila, can I take a look at the ship scans of Yvette's ship from the security checks when she docked?"

Gila nodded, "Meet me at the command chamber in thirty minutes and we can go over them. Lance, I think you know where most of these supplies are stored. Will you begin to put this away while I assist your father?"

Lance smiled up at Gila, "By me? SURE!"

Martin led Joe down the long passageway to the sleeping quarters. While picking out individual bunks, Martin thought about how much he was looking forward to a shower and a shave. From what he had seen, Lance was doing well, but was Lance safe here? A ship had been stolen from this very station. Thinking back to the ships he had seen around Venus made him wonder what sort of outfit was roaming around in this neck of the woods. Martin had never been the type to ignore red flags, but usually they didn't show up this late in the game. He had a real choice to make. The next portion of the run was the most dangerous. Once his collectors were sent out, he would only be able to monitor them remotely. Calling off the run might be prudent, but it would cost him. Was he willing to risk his family's financial future on the possibility that sending out his collectors would make him a target?

* * * * *

The days passed very quickly on the solar observatory. There was a lot to see, and many things needed to be done before the launching of the collectors. One week hardly seemed enough time to get everything in order. Martin, Joe, and Yvette sat in the records room, reviewing all of the computer from the time of the crime for the twentieth time while Lance was in the hall tending to a large terrarium. "It doesn't make any sense!" exclaimed Martin. "Even if someone hacked your ship Yvette, how could the signal have gotten through SOHOIII's shielding? The comms connection might have allowed access, but comms systems are always independent of main ship computers because they are so vulnerable. Someone would have had to have been on-board your ship, but all the scans of the White Nova come up negative for a lifeform.

"Now you can see why Gila and I have no explanation for this. We tracked the ship to the perimeter of our tracking capabilities, and it appeared to be on a rendezvous course with another ship. The trajectory of my ship's path would take it toward Venus." said Yvette.

"You know, we noticed a lot of activity around Venus," remarked Martin. Lance, who had been listening intently stepped into the room,

"Ya! I was actually fired on near Venus," he said.

Martin froze as he processed what his son had just said, his complexion turning deathly white as his face drained of blood. "Someone fired at you near Venus?"

"I was just going past the planet, and I noticed the same thing. A lot of activity and I knew that the project to colonize had been canceled some time ago. All of a sudden, I was in the middle of target practice, and I was the bull's eye!"

"WHAT?!" Just as quickly, the blood flooded back to Martin's face as if a bomb at his core had exploded. Martin was on his feet. He couldn't handle this news. Why had no body told him?

Lance had jumped up too. "Dad I'm ok. The pod got me out." Lance answered. "It's amazing! It's got a shield and it's crazy fast! Years ahead of what's on your ship... The cloaking device didn't work, but it still got me out."

Yvette's eyes had widened at Martin's anger. She was watching him pace the room. "We notified the security dispatch about that incident as well, Martin. When Lance arrived, he was a little banged up, but nothing too bad. Sorry we didn't tell you sooner."

Martin walked over and hugged his son, "What am I going to do with you kid?"

Lance blushed. Then after a few seconds, he noticed Yvette watching them and he pushed Martin away saying, "C'mon dad."

"I did manage to engage the homing device before my ship got out of range," continued Yvette.

"It's a starting point anyway. Nothing else worked. Not the remote pilot, the self-destruct or any other command transmitted to the White Nova. I believe my homing device worked because it was not linked to the main computer. It was my own instrumentation, privately installed."

"Whoever has your ship might have had enough time to remove the collectors and dispose of it, in which case nothing will be recovered. I'll help if I can," said Marty.

"And of course, you can count on me!" toned Joe.

"Thank you, Martin. I truly appreciate your expert advice." Yvette glared at Joe when she said the word "expert". She had made it more than apparent that Joe's help was unwanted. Yvette got up. "Lance wants to get something to eat? Are you guys going to be at this for a while longer?"

Martin frowned, "No, I don't think we can ignore the facts on this one. Something or someone was on your ship, Yvette."

Yvette just shook her head and then left with Lance for the kitchen.

"So, have you ever heard of a ship being stolen like this?" asked Joe.

"Not without any evidence of another person on board. This is the first time I've heard of anything like this," answered Martin.

"How is the investigation going?" asked Gila as he entered the room.

"Not well," answered Martin.

"Any idea how soon you'll be able to launch your collectors?" the biosystem asked.

"Wanting to get rid of us, huh?" joked Marty.

Gila frowned. "No, you know that's not true, you're always welcome here, friend. I am just looking forward to the rest. I've never had such a long-term guest as Ms. Yvette. You were not here when her ship was exiting. I feared for my life, to say the least."

"Actually," continued Martin, smiling inspite of himself, "the collectors will launch tomorrow and as soon they're retrieved, we'll all be gone." He could only imagine the scene between Gila and rampaging Yvette as they tried to stop White Nova's theft. SOHOIII was fully equipped with defensive capabilities. The station was designed with the understanding that it would off of the beaten path and vulnerable due to reduced frequency of security patrols this sector. What the station did lack was personnel. The thieves of White Nova took advantage of automation of station resulting Gila and Yvette being too late to manually lock down the station's superior shielding, keeping the ship inside. Yvette immediately began attempting to access the ship remotely. When that failed, she turned attempting to disable the ship with the station's primary cannons. The White Nova's propulsion systems were still functional after two hits but it was obvious to Yvette that a third might very well destroy the ship and the collectors it held internally and so she made the choice allow the ship to be taken. Yvette's frustration even now was tangible and explosive, state that all of the humans on the station understood. Martin could only wonder if Gila, with his isolation, had ever been around human dealing with crisis situation like this one.

Gila nodded.

"I have always resisted additional attempts to increase the population of both humans and biosystems on SOHOIII. This is mainly because I have observed that I work more efficiently with my solitude, but in light of recent events, perhaps I will need to reconsider bringing on an assistant."

Joe had been marveling at all of Gila's projects. "I don't know how you find the time to work on all this research and take care of the solar telescope, the magnetometer, the station, and monitor all the docking and landing activities," he said.

Gila was in his element. "The solar telescope is technically not maintained by me. I have worked on it a few times in the past for different projects, but the telescope is remotely controlled from Earth and the servicing missions are only necessary about once every five years or so. The station is equipped to continuously check all the systems and structures for flaws, and then creates a priority list for me to follow up on routinely. The docking and launching require a little coordinating. Actually, the computer does much of that, as well, but obviously there are flaws in the automation that will need to be addressed."

"Sounds like a busy schedule to me. When do you have time to work on your research?" asked Joe.

"Hmmm... I do not set time aside to work on my projects. I set time aside to perform the mundane tasks necessary for the maintenance of this station. My experimentation will always be the higher priority. When necessary, I can request an assist team to take care of the station if my work leaves me no additional time, but that has only ever occurred twice. Generally, I prefer to forgo sleep, rather than bring on additional help."

"Wow really? How long can you go without sleep?" asked Joe.

"In my current state, I can forgo sleeping for approximately fifty Earth days. If my experimentation allows me to reduce my metabolic rate, I can triple that. However, if I intend to not sleep, there are strict dietary restrictions that I must be prepared for ahead of time, which makes up some of the supplies you brought me."

"That's incredible! It sounds like you've made yourself quite a home here Gila." Martin wasn't surprised that Joe was so impressed by Gila. During Gila's development, he attracted quite a bit of attention due to his incredible aptitude for nearly all STEM subjects. The attention was not all positive, however. Several groups began to advocate that creating biosystems with such advanced intelligence levels was dangerous. But so far biosystems like Gila and PoPo had not given their creators any real cause for concern. Martin's opinion had always been that while a biosystem can be ambitious, their values have always been different from humans. Most of the regulations that are in place for biosystem creation are to ensure that the motives behind the human scientists are not questionable and to ensure that the responsibilities of the creators are being upheld. Biosystems seem to just want to live their lives and that is something Martin understood. If one day, they view world domination or omnicide as their principal motive, then that seems more of a failure on the human side of the equation.

"The station didn't always look like it does now. I've molded it to my idea of a home, and what you see around you are my children. Lives I have created through genetics. They may not be biologically linked to me, but I love them as any parent would love their own. My plants, in return, give me life as well, through their oxygen by-products and food sustenance." Gila remarked.

"Aren't you capable of producing your own oxygen?" asked Joe.

"Of course, but the station is also prepared to support additional life. There would be an occasional strain on the supply without the extra help." commented Gila.

Joe continued to pepper Gila with questions until Gila abruptly called a stop as some internal timer called him away for one of his projects. Martin was going to check in on the preparations for the collectors' launch and Joe decided he should get his badly needed shut eye.

Joe passed Yvette's door on the way to his sleeping quarters and stopped.

He wasn't sure if she had finished eating but gave it a shot and knocked. "Come in," was the reply. She was sitting on her bunk with her back against the wall, reading from an optical computer with a small glass and a silver flask on the mounted shelf that acted as a nightstand.

"I, uh didn't mean to bother you, I just wanted to stop by and talk to you, if you were still up." Joe said awkwardly.

Yvette dimmed her optical computer, "Talk to me about what?"

"I just wanted to tell you I was sorry if I came on too strong earlier. I admire the fact that you're a pilot, and from what I hear, a damn good one. I actually haven't met many women runners."

Yvette snorted ever so slightly, her expression more than a little disbelieving, but the slight turn of her lips suggested a smile. "Grab a glass," she tilted her head indicating the stack of small glasses next to the sink. Joe picked up one of the glasses and slid a trunk from the corner over to the make-shift nightstand. Yvette poured each of them some of the vodka from her flask. "My co-pilot ditched me on this run. She just got engaged, so last minute she decides she should not come. I thought about canceling the run. In fact, I was stupid not to, as it turns out."

"Well, hindsight is twenty-twenty." Joe raised his glass and said, "Nah zda rovh yeh." He had taken some Russian at the academy. He tipped back his vodka. It was fairly smooth, but some still managed to go down the wrong pipe, sending him into a coughing fit. "For me right now, my hindsight is telling me I shouldn't have tried to breathe while I drink. Who knew?"

Yvette rolled her eyes. "I see the appeal. If you could breathe while drinking, think of all the brain cells you could save when you take those really long gulps."

"It's a legitimate concern. Might just be enough to counter-act the ones I'm losing from the vodka itself," said Joe as he tried to recover from the embarrassment of choking on his drink.

Yvette's smile was a little more open this time as she lifted her flask. "More?"

Joe set his glass down for her to pour, "Is this your first run by yourself then?"

"My first hydrogen run alone, but I've done quite a few supply drop-offs to different stations. It's why I'm here, actually. The supply shipment was too large for the White Nova, so it looks like they had you guys bring in the second half."

"So, you've been a pilot for a while then? Wait, Karrnoff are you related to Anatoly Karrnoff?" It wasn't completely unusual to have a pilot with as much experience as Yvette being so young. The flight academy Joe attended wasn't the only way to receive training and it just clicked for Joe that she may have had one hell of a teacher.

"Yes, he's my grandfather." Yvette sighed. Thinking about her grandfather instantly depressed her.

"I'm sure he'll understand about all this, Yvette. He was one of the first hydrogen runners. I bet he's seen some worse scenarios than even this one. So, Anatoly Karrnoff trained you, huh? I bet your parents loved that..." Joe had meant it sarcastically, but Yvette downed her vodka and started pouring herself another glass.

"They would have hated it," she said.

"Would have?" asked Joe.

"My grandfather and I only had each other after my parents died in a crash when I was ten. Grandfather wasn't around at the beginning, and it was extremely hard on both of us. I hated the schools he sent me too. They always felt more like prisons. When I showed interest in becoming a pilot the pieces just seemed to fit. He would take me on his safer missions, and he taught me everything he knew about being a pilot. I loved it, and now I guess I can't stand to disappoint him."

Joe knew his face hardened after hearing her story. He had been staring at his vodka glass. Her story was too similar to his own. He had always avoided talking about his parents, which generally meant he avoid talking about why he loved to fly. It was too easy to feel how Yvette was feeling right now. Maybe that is why his subconscious started to employ a defense mechanism or two.

Yvette seemed surprised by the cold turn in his demeanor, but she smiled and handled it with grace. "You're launching your collectors tomorrow. You need your sleep."

Joe nodded, "Thanks for the drink." He left the room without drinking his second glass of vodka. He was halfway down the hall when he heard a soft, "good luck" come from Yvette's room.

* * * * *

Launch day finally arrived with all the hustle of a major liftoff at the Space Center on Earth. Martin and Joe began systems checks early in the morning and were finally ready to launch their collectors. They would then be sealing themselves inside the control room, as there had to be 24-hour surveillance on the collectors. Pilots who did this alone had to set alarms for every hour and generally did it all from the cockpit of their ship. It was a nerve-racking time and possibly the hardest part of the whole thing. Martin was really glad to have Joe along with him at this part!

"Thank you, Yvette for all your help." Martin said. She had been remarkable in helping them prepare. It was great having another seasoned pilot to assist in the details.

"It was my pleasure," she answered, "The sooner you're done, the sooner I can get home."

"Lance, you stay out here and help Gila." Martin said to his son.

"I could help you, Dad." said Lance.

Martin could only grin at this. Something about space seemed to really bring that spark out of Lance. He was always locked away in his room at home, but up here, he was an excited member of the team. If this was the bright side of the entire fiasco with his son, then Martin was starting to believe it was worth it. A big part of him wanted his son in that command room with him and Joe, but he knew that right now the stakes were high, and the tension was not going to make for a good bonding experience. He gripped Lance's shoulder appreciating his son's strong locked gaze. "There's going to be a time for that Lance. I'm going to make sure of it, but today I need you to leave this to just me and Joe." Lance sighed and nodded, relief and disappointment mixing in his expression.

"Let's get inside, Joe!" Martin hollered.

"I'm ther,." came Joe's reply. "The launch systems on all the collectors are primed."

The collectors were the engineering marvels that made runs possible. Once they were released, a funnel opened up to help collect the hydrogen ions. The sides of the funnel were negatively charged to help attract the fuel. The main base of the collectors had a stronger negative charge so the hydrogen atoms wouldn't stick to the funnel, but instead, flow into the base. They had a programmable flight plan so they could be directed into the most concentrated areas of the flare. Once a collector filled up, the funnel would retract, and their homing device steers the container back to the runner's ship. The ship has temperature-controlled stalls that store the collectors. Over time, the hydrogen in the collectors liquefies, allowing the container to shrink in size and be more manageable for the pilot. These stalls prevented the tanks from getting too hot or from moving around on re-entry. Of course, many things could go astray on such complicated devices. The collectors might be hit by space debris, the flare itself could cause the collector to catch fire, the funnels could fail to deploy or retract, or the homing device might not activate properly. Just to name a few. On a typical run, Martin would lose 3 or 4 collectors due to these failures but, the majority made it back. There was always the nefarious chance that someone in the area would help themselves to a full container, which would necessitate other actions.

A standard-sized solar flare releases millions of tons of charged particles. The particle density of a flare can vary depending on its temperature and energy. Each one is slightly different. An exceptionally large flare can contain billions of tons of particles and release large amounts of electromagnetic energy. The electronics and the batteries of running all the systems of the containers had to be shielded against the electromagnetics released. Engineering was challenged to the extreme, but once these collectors became available, Earth entered a new era in energy production.

Martin nodded to Joe and turned to the control console, "We have Gila's clearance for launch. Begin countdown."

"Sixty seconds to launch. Fifty-seven seconds to launch." Came the countdown numbers over the speaker system.

"Get ready for the worst part," Martin mumbled to Joe.

"So far, this isn't in the same league as bedhead," grinned Joe.

"Launch ignition!" shouted the speaker system.

"Looks good! All the collectors have ignited successfully and they're off!" said an excited Joe. It was a textbook launch. Now they had to wait the two weeks it would take for the solar collectors to do their job, and for them to return home.

"Their course looks good so far," said Joe.

"Yeah, they're doing fine for now, but I won't be happy until these puppies are loaded onto the Texas Star, and we're bound for home." answered Martin.

"I'm going to take the first shift. Any problem with that?" asked Martin as he settled in to observe the preset trajectory paths of the various collectors.

"No, I'll just try to get some sleep. I seem to be really tired since the stasis," replied Joe.

Martin looked at Joe curiously but didn't say anything. He turned to the controls and began his work on the guidance system. If he could catch the flares just right, he knew that this could be his last run. The thought of retirement depressed him, but with Lance's interest in space, maybe retirement meant he could mentor his son. Nicole would likely kill him if he wrapped Lance up in hydrogen running, but that did not seem like Lance's calling. It would be important for Lance to learn some piloting skills if he planned to work out in space and it was something Martin could look forward to. Pushing his son out of his thoughts, Martin focused back on the status of the collectors, regularly inputting the calculations for their estimated time of arrival for the hydrogen catch and adjusting their course as needed.

* * * * *

Day by day, Martin and Joe worked in shifts. They would sit for a few hours, then sleep, and maybe do some reading. It had taken Joe a few days to work up the courage to finally talk to Yvette again, but SOHOIII was not large, and he ran into her often. Gila and Lance were wrapped up in the wet lab and Martin was sleeping when Yvette walked in on Joe in the kitchen frying up a batch of his semi-famous-as-it-was-known-by-at-least-three-different-roommates-from-the-academy, fried rice. He looked up again and with his most charming smile asked,

"Hungry?"

She smiled, "It smells good. Sure!"

* * * * *

"Martin can I have a word with you?" inquired Gila.

"Sure, what's on your mind?" Answered Martin, diverting his attention from the computer screens for a while.

"It's about Lance. You see, I have had an intern position available from the agency for quite a while now but haven't been able to fill it because the right person hasn't been there for me. I would like to offer this position to Lance. If you are ok with that," replied Gila.

"How long would he be working here at the station, and what about his schoolwork?" Martin wondered.

"The position is for a minimum of a year but then, that is if the intern works out, it can be shortened. The position is open-ended since the help is always needed and as for his schoolwork, I can tutor him and administer the exams as needed. The experience he would get working in the labs and mastering all the scientific equipment would be very valuable to him in the future," explained Gila.

"I'm ok with this arrangement if Lance wants to do it. I'll leave it up to the 2 of you and of course I'll have to let his mother know about this situation and see what she thinks about it," replied Martin.

"Great!" said Gila, hardly able to contain his delight in the possibility of having a worthwhile assistant. "I'll get back to you after talking to Lance about this." He continued smiling broadly.

Two weeks were gone as Martin continued to check his readings. "Perfect!" he shouted. "This is definitely my best haul to date! Let's bring 'em in!"

Joe came over to the control desk. He marveled at the blips on the screen and how significant they were to the existence of life on earth.

"What the..." Martin's words broke the silence. "The collectors are veering off course!" Martin rapidly entered commands into the computer. "They're not responding!"

"What do you want me to do?" asked Joe, anxiously.

"Jesus! They're not even taking manual commands. I've tried destroying one of the pods!" said Martin.

"That's exactly what happened to Yvette's ship!" remarked Joe. "I know we did a thorough check of the pods!"

"These collectors were never checked so many times in all my days of running! There's no way the self-destruct mechanism shouldn't work!" shouted Martin.

"Let me try to re-route them and if necessary, destroy them," volunteered Joe.

"Okay, let's try to make a random course alteration," said Martin.

"Nothing," came the reply from Joe.

"Activate self-destructs on all of them," said Martin.

"Nothing again."

"Open the room, I'm going to get Gila's roundabout and go get one of those pods myself," said Martin.

"I'll do the space walk. I need the experience." said Joe.

"Okay, get suited up. I'll pilot the ship and work the robotic arm. Hopefully, you won't have to go out, but I'm not coming back empty-handed." said Martin.

The two left the control center at a dead run. They made the necessary arrangements with the roundabout and said rapid "goodbyes" to the others at SOHOIII. Lance watched from the viewing screen as his father and Joe sped off toward the sun. He felt both fear and exhilaration as he saw them struggle against the extreme force of the solar winds. He turned to see Yvette, outwardly calm, but with small, white knuckles gripping the back of the chair she was kneeling in. He closed his eyes, and as he had done so many times before, and wished for his father's safe return.

CHAPTER 8

THE RECOVERY

"We should intercept the first of the collectors in about an hour and then hopefully, we can grab it." Martin explained to Joe as they checked the systems inside the cockpit. Joe was dressed in the spacewalk outfit just in case he would have to venture outside. "I sure hope we can grab it with the arm. This area of space is a son of a bitch. You'll lose radiation protection by going outside and the solar winds can play havoc when you're trying to do any kind of movement. I'll try to keep the ship between you and the sun to provide extra radiation protection. Every little bit a shielding helps, so stay in the shadow of the ship."

"Do you have any idea how this is happening?" asked Joe.

"Not really. I've never seen anything like this," came the reply. "There was mention of it on the Internet that an Australian and Japanese runner had had some collectors stolen, but there wasn't any real explanation as to how it had happened. No, the only way we'll be able to find out what happened is to analyze one of these unresponsive collectors ourselves."

Time passed excruciatingly slow, allowing the tension and anxiety to build. "There it is," Marty finally said. "I'm going in with the arm first and hopefully avoid a spacewalk. Okay, we're almost there. Extending...okay, I've got it, I'm closing the catch."

Joe watched tensely and jumped as the collector slipped from the grip of the arm. "Try it again, Marty," he said.

"I'm aligning the arm again. I got it!" Once again, the collector slipped out of the arm.

"Dammit!" he yelled. "The solar winds are kicking my ass out there!"

"Okay, I'm going out. If we don't get that collector, we're going to lose it altogether." Joe said, jumping up from his seat. The motion of the ship caused him to lose his balance temporarily. He got his bearings back and reached for the air lock.

"Good luck kid. I'll realign the arm, but I'll wait for your okay to close the catch. Move slowly and watch out for that wind. Make sure you are attached to the pod; I don't want to have to catch you too." advised Martin.

"It's kind of like jumping into a pool for the first time, hoping you can swim," said Joe, grinning. He was trying to make light of the situation, but it was a frightening exercise. Astronauts had been sucked into the sun, never to be seen again doing very similar things.

The air lock was very small. It hardly allowed room for Joe and the bulky suit he was wearing. Joe kept trying to remember all the steps required in the simulated space walk on Earth. One forgotten procedure and this could be his first and only walk. As the air lock opened into the large expanse of space, Joe felt himself hyperventilating and barely able to move. He also became painfully aware of the intense heat emanating from the ship. He was finally able to feel around on the exterior for the attachment where he needed to lock in his harness.

"Woah! Try to relax out there," admonished Martin. He could see Joe starting to panic when he couldn't make contact with the connector to his suit. That was the most dangerous thing about a spacewalk. Feeling like you were out of control and all alone. He started worrying when Joe's breathing appeared erratic on the monitor. He had to calm the young pilot down.

"I'll be okay, Marty. I got the buckle. I just got overwhelmed out here, for a minute."

"I can certainly understand that Joe. You're doing great now. Go slow..."

"Man!" exclaimed Joe, "The surface is really hot, even through the suit. I can feel the electrical charges flying all around me! It's a really strange feeling! I'll have it in a minute."

"Take your time, Joe. I can see you on the exterior viewer. You're doing great. Keep talking to me if you can." Martin could sense Joe's nervous fear.

"Okay, I'm at the arm. Guiding it around..."

Martin realized that he, himself was not breathing. The suspense of watching Joe's every move was building. He saw the young man sway against the solar wind and then try to steady himself against the hot surface of the ship only to yank his hand away from the heat.

Soon Joe was back on the arm, working his way toward the collector. In their storage state, the collectors were roughly the size of a small tank. Once filled, however, they expanded to the size of 20' X 5', approximately. The hydrogen would soon be frozen, allowing the collectors to return to the more manageable size. Each collector, if full would yield nearly three million dollars for the pilot. Joe would be allowed one of these collectors, to tide him over until his next run. Martin had taken on one extra for just that reason. Because Joe was young and single, he would be able to make another run in no time at all.

Martin's attention was drawn back to the drama outside the ship. "Jesus!" shouted Joe as he just barely missed the collector. "Okay, I've got it. Close the catch, Martin."

"We got it!" said Martin as he heard the encouraging "thud" of the clamp. "Get back in the ship!" he said to Joe.

"You don't have to tell me that twice!" he answered back. Martin's eyes flickered back and forth between the collector and Joe as he made his way painstakingly back. He'd gone too far to screw it up now!

"Okay, I'm in the lock!" shouted Joe.

"Gotcha!" answered Martin as he closed the airlock. "Retracting the arm, this baby is in the hold."

"We did it!" Joe was at Martin's side by now, his helmet in his hands and a huge grin on his face.

"You did a great job out there, kid," said Martin appreciatively.

"Oh, I'm all set for another. When do I go?" Joe said sarcastically.

"Ha! Let's get back to SOHOIII and have a look at this one. See what's up with it," replied Martin.

Silently, Joe murmured a "Thank God that's over," as his knees went just the slightest bit weak. He looked up to Martin. He didn't dare let the older man see his fear and relief.

Neither man spoke on the return to the space station. Joe was exhausted from his lack of sleep and a very draining spacewalk. He fell in and out of sleep, jumping at the slightest change in movement. Martin was too lost in thought to attempt a conversation. He was anxious to get back and dig into the collector. The docking pad was before him in no time. He nudged Joe, gently to prepare him for the landing.

Wake up, buddy."

"Oh. okay," said Joe, dazed and a bit uncertain as he shook off the sleepiness. Martin's landing was clean. They tethered the ship and removed the collector from the hold. Gila had placed a forklift on the dock for the transfer of the collector. He and Yvette were waiting inside for them as they entered. "Amazing spacewalk, Joe!" he said.

"We watched it all from the telescope." said Yvette. "You did a perfect job."

"Yeah, well, it's been the many years of experience that prepared me," joked Joe.

"I don't mean to be rude, but I want to get into this thing right away so that I might have a chance to salvage some of the others." said Martin. "Do you have an area where I might be able to totally disassemble this, Gila?"

"Of course. Just inside the second landing bay, is a large platform. I'll fetch you some tables to put together and a few tools that I have laying around." With that, the little biosystem was off.

"Could you also get me a tank to transfer this hydrogen into?" asked Martin.

"Sure," said Gila, over his shoulder.

"Thanks." he answered.

"What a haul this would have been." Martin said more to himself than anyone else.

Gila soon had everything arranged, and the collector was perched on the table. Joe, Yvette, Gila and Lance watched in silence. Martin began speaking his findings.

"The wire to the transmitter source for the computer has been cut and the self-destruct apparatus has been disconnected. I can see where the switch activating the self-destruct mechanism was flipped on, but because the mechanism was disconnected it didn't power up."

Joe moved in to look at what Martin was talking about. "The cut on the wires aren't clean. They look like they've been bitten through or eaten at by an acidic solution," he commented.

"Yeah, I agree," said Martin, "But how is that possible since I had control of the collectors until they entered the flare? Then there was too much radiation once they got near the flare for me to check any systems or issue any commands. They weren't cut up to that point!" Martin thought for a minute and then said, "Maybe, a temperature-activated chemical was placed on the wires that ate through them once they reached their destination."

"No, that couldn't be it, because we would have picked up any foreign chemicals in our systems check. Besides, how would anyone have found the time to take these collectors apart to place the compound on the proper areas?" asked Joe.

"You're right. Someone must have re-programmed the computer just before entering the flare and just before the wires were disconnected," answered Martin.

"But how could that have happened?" asked Joe.

"I don't know.... did anyone pick up another ship in this vicinity?" asked Martin.

"No, and I've been monitoring this area very closely, watching for whoever intercepted my ship," said Yvette.

Gila had been relatively silent up to this point. He finally said, "Would you mind if I had a look?"

"Of course not," replied Martin.

"I just need to go get some of my tools from my laboratory and my portable microscope from the greenhouse."

"I'll get your microscope," volunteered Lance.

"Great. I'll be back in a moment with my tools," said Gila. Martin, Yvette, and Joe continued to study the collector until the other two returned.

"What is it you suspect?" Martin asked Gila.

"Okay, well this might sound ridiculous, but if you follow the sequence of events, there had to be someone or something on board those collectors!"

"You're right," answered Marty. "It does sound ridiculous. We would have picked up any foreign body inside these pods, but everything checked out. I did the check myself, not just once but several times this trip. More times than on any run I've ever been on in fact."

"Suppose the foreign body was microscopic. Your scanners would have missed it, right?" asked Gila while grabbing the microscope from Lance's hand as he returned out of breath to the landing bay.

"Well, yes, that's true. The detectors don't pick up any foreign chemicals or biomass less than two micrograms. We would need more accurate detectors for smaller amounts of contaminants, and that's really unheard of."

"Exactly my point. I think there is a distinct possibility that we're dealing with microscopic biosystems. I've heard of some work being done in that area..."

Lance quietly left the bay for a second time. He went to "his" pod and quickly retrieved the research notes he had found there. "Here," he said, barely able to breathe this time and handing the notes to Gila. "I found these on board the pod I took. Maybe they'll be easier for you to understand."

"My oh, my!" gasped Gila as he looked through the notes. "Someone has been doing very extensive research on micro-biosystems, and apparently has had some success!"

"What do you mean?" asked Martin. "I don't understand what all of this has to do with my collectors."

"Well, Marty, micro-biosystems are simply miniatures of regular biosystems like me and Apollowalla. They are intelligent organisms with the ability to carry on certain functions. They were originally thought of for productive reasons... mechanical repair, medical improvements, security systems...But then came the fear that they might be used in a destructive manner, so much of the research became top secret and not supported in academia. It would appear that someone, however, continued their studies, and actually created some."

"I still don't know..." continued Martin.

"I'm getting there. Suppose these extremely small systems were planted in the collectors and they remained dormant until the collectors were launched. Their first task was probably to disconnect the self-destruct mechanism." Gila replied.

"I've never heard of such a thing!" said Joe.

"That's because these procedures are very new and extremely delicate. All I have to do is obtain some scrapings in the area where the wires were broken and place them on a slide." Gila said, setting up his microscope. He then proceeded to do just that. He took scrapings from all over the collector and placed them on numerous slides. After several minutes of placing slides on the stand, he finally said, "Here it is."

"What?" asked Martin anxiously.

"Take a look at these cells. They once belonged to a living entity, which was bred for one function. To disconnect two wires. This biosystem had a one-way ticket on this trip. Once its task was accomplished, it could not survive the harsh conditions in the flare."

"That's sick!" said Joe. "So, someone is using these creatures for an evil purpose, and then sending them on suicide missions."

"I find it appalling, as well," said Gila.

"These systems could really be of great use to us if they weren't abused," continued Lance.

"True, but for now, we need to find out who's doing them wrong!" answered Martin.

"I can bet you that these creatures had something to do with the disappearance of my ship as well." said Yvette.

"We need to leave right away. We might be able to catch up with some of the lost collectors and follow whoever picks them up," said Joe.

"What are we waiting for?" asked Yvette.

"How soon can we be ready for launch?" continued Joe.

"It'll take me about thirty minutes. Grab everything you need to load aboard the Texas Star and let's get this show on the road. I'll need your help with the launch, Gila." said Martin.

"Glad to be of assistance any way I can," he replied.

"You can count on my help, too, Dad," said Lance. Martin smiled at his son.

"I know Lance. I'll need you to give Gila a few breaks as he monitors us in space. You're more than capable. I know." Lance beamed. For the first time in his life, his dad had shown faith in him. The effect was amazing. The young man nearly skipped to the control room behind Gila. Martin shook his head and laughed softly to himself.

"I'm ready to board!" said Yvette, two small suitcases in hand.

"I don't mean this in a sexist way, but my goodness, you pack lightly and quickly for a woman!" said Martin.

"I fly pretty good for a chick, too!" she said sarcastically. Seconds behind her came Joe.

"I'm ready," he said.

"Give me a minute or two, you guys get loaded and I'll be right behind you," said Martin. Within minutes, everyone and everything were on board and the launch clearance had been given. The countdown had been started. "Lance?" Martin said to his son over the radio, "Would you update your mother, please?"

"Oh sure, Dad, leave the dirty work to me. You know she's gonna wig!"

"You can handle it!" Marty replied.

"...Seven... Six..." the countdown continued.

"Jesus, this is the fastest I've ever performed launch sequence checks," commented Joe.

"You and me, both!" laughed Martin.

"...Two...One...Liftoff!" "Good luck and keep us informed!" shouted Gila.

"Thanks, Gila!" shouted Martin over the din. "And thanks also for looking after Lance. He'll be much safer there with you and will make a wonderful assistant. Did you tell him about the offer yet?"

"I'm about to, Martin. Have a safe trip."

"Let the chase begin." said Yvette. "Also, here are the frequency numbers for the homing device on my ship."

"That's great. We can scan this area for your ship and any remaining collectors that just might be floating around. We managed to get 8 collectors back. About half of them. But where did the others end up??" said Martin.

"Hey, Marty, Yvette, take a look at this." said Joe, pointing to the screen.

"It looks like three of our collectors! Let's get 'em!" said Martin. As Joe pointed the craft in the direction of the collectors, Martin said, "Wait, a minute... On second thought, let's just pick up two of them, and follow the third."

The arm on the Texas Star was more maneuverable than the one on the roundabout, and the two collectors were much easier to retrieve with the bigger ship. They had the two renegade collectors on board in no time.

"Great job, Marty," said Joe. "Do you want us to take these two apart as well?"

"No, we don't have any extra containers for the Hydrogen. But you could run a detailed scan of them just to make sure there's no little hitchhikers that survived. Hey, we're only short five more collectors, and we're following one of them. Maybe we can make some profit on this trip after all!"

"So where do you think these guys are heading? A mother ship?" asked Joe.

"Not sure, really, but that would be my guess. There is a chance she might have already gone, not realizing she left these collectors behind. If that's the case, a ship that size should be pretty easy to find, and not too far away. We'll have to stay out of detection range but use radiation signatures to follow far behind. I'm going to take a wild guess and say that our pirate ship is heading toward Venus."

"What makes you say that?" asked Yvette.

"We saw so much activity there when we went past it on our way to SOHOIII, and I'm assuming that there's more going on than meets the eye." Martin answered.

It wasn't long before another ship was picked up on the sensors.

"There she is, Joe!" shouted Martin. Just a small blip indicating another ship showed on the edge of the screen. "We'll stop here, let it pick up the last collector, and then follow her in. I can put a lock on her radiation trail and the automatic pilot can keep us on course. You two go down below and start clearing some cargo space for the collectors. I'm going to be optimistic and think we're going get them all back."

"Why don't you be optimistic for both of us, and believe that we'll get my ship back as well?" said Yvette.

"Of course," said Martin. "And don't worry. I'll stay on this jerk's tail. He has five of my collectors, and I was beginning to think I might retire on this shipment." Yvette and Joe went down the narrow stairs to the cargo hold. Their arms brushed against each other, and they were once again drawn into the visual embrace of distant lovers. "I don't intend to let you walk out of my life once we've recovered your ship, you know." said Joe.

"Nor I, you," answered Yvette.

"Please say that you'll come to the United States with me. You know I don't speak Russian," smiled Joe.

"What about a neutral country, where there's no turmoil, like New Zealand?" she countered.

"We'll see. It is beautiful there," answered Joe. The two kissed briefly and then began the chore of putting the storage area back in shape.

Back upstairs, Martin was thinking out loud, "This guy is making it too easy to follow him. He must have a small oil leak since I'm also picking up oil droplets in the vapor trail." Martin was looking through the computer to find out everything he could about the Venus station, aside from what Lance had observed. The space consortium had started the project several years earlier. Because of the high winds, corrosive atmosphere and temperatures on Venus, everything planned as an underground establishment with only a few, heavily re-enforced out buildings. Aside from the extensive scientific center that was planned, it was also going to act as a relay station and storage facility for waste products and weapons. Several private contractors had also put in bids to establish a long-term prison there. Due to the expense of the transport, the prisoners would have to be serving a sentence of forty years or more and were extremely violent or habitual offenders. These things were fairly convenient public knowledge, but what Martin couldn't determine was how far from the construction had gone before building was halted. He suspected that the pirate ship was to rendezvous with someone either in the vicinity of Venus or at the actual station itself, based on all the activity he had experienced while passing by the big planet.

"So, this is where they chose to put the station..." Martin said to himself, looking at a crude map of Venus. "It would only make sense to use the existing mountain range and to build the station into the side of Maxwell Buttes, the largest of the peaks." They had actually completed the second stage of construction, which meant that it was virtually finished. The concrete foundation and radioactive storage facilities had all been completed. The final stage of construction involved installing all the temperature control devices. Painting, putting in appliances, light fixtures, water purifiers and oxygen generators, was all that was needed to finish the station. Essentially making the station ready for whoever wanted to take it over. However, the environment on Venus was too toxic on the surface which upped the cost of the construction and did not allow its completion.

Venus is a perfect hideout for anyone with illegal goods or performing illegal acts. No one in their right mind would bother with such a place. The bunkers would be very hard to penetrate with conventional sensors and the distance of the planet provided sanctuary for wrongdoers. However, there was a very large ship hiding behind Venus, flying in sequence with the planet. This very large ship was the size of a small station and if it maintained its orbit could not be viewed from Earth. It was on the dark side of the planet so to speak. "Why didn't someone anticipate this situation?" mused Martin. He shook his head and quietly began to ponder the possibilities that lay ahead.

CHAPTER 9

VENUS

Martin continued to examine the design of the Venus ship in the hope that he might find a way to quickly get in and out with the stolen belongings. Slowly, a plan of attack began to form. He called to Joe and Yvette. When they reached his area, he began to tell them his thoughts. "I have come to the conclusion, as I told you before that this very large ship hidden behind Venus is being used by these criminals who are stealing from everyone in the solar system. I'm certain that when we get in there, we'll find a lot of missing collectors. Yvette's ship has to be somewhere in the region. That is if they haven't already disassembled it for parts."

"Or they could be using it to pick up pirated collectors," Yvette added.

"I would think that the stolen collectors might be stored here," said Martin, pointing to a large circular area on one side of the ship.

"We might have a chance if we can get someone near this air lock just above it without being noticed," speculated Martin.

"You're making an awfully big assumption, here, Marty. What makes you think that there's only one place to store those collectors? This place looks mammoth!" said Joe.

"I've looked this ship over and over. That's the only place big enough to store collectors in stalls. I'm going to send Gila an image of this thing and see if he has any suggestions. He has better sensor and imaging computers that I have here. But no matter what, we got to get someone out there," answered Martin.

"That's assuming we can shield someone long enough to work outside," said Yvette.

"Yes, but the airlock is currently on the shaded side of the ship. We can just hope they don't rotate or move out of position. Logically speaking, there is only one place to put huge Hydrogen tanks with stalls!" replied Martin.

"So, what's your plan of attack, commander?" asked Joe.

"Well, as I see it, there's only one way we can do this. We'll need to get into that ship, where we believe they're storing the collectors. I can work in the Texas Star alone to load collectors while you release them and make your way back over then we will leave as soon as possible. I'm getting a response back from Gila. That was fast," answered Martin. Response "I FOUND IT!" yelled Gila.

"Found what?" Martin responded.

"Yvette's ship! I can just make it out towards the rear and there appears to be another ship moored nearby. That, I'll bet is the Kitty Hawk you talked about," explained Gila, excited that he could help them out.

"Wow, thank you so much. Yvette is throwing you a kiss right now." grinned Martin.

"Keep me informed and SOHIII is standing by if we can be of any further assistance. Over," said Gila as he signed off.

"I would guess that there aren't very many of these people involved. Perhaps just a handful," mused Yvette.

"What makes you say that?" asked Joe.

"Simple. They would have to have an extensive life support system in place to sustain a fair number of people on such a large ship. Plus more electricity, more activity, more attention. They are trying to be discreet, remember?" she answered.

"Then how do you explain both the Texas Star and Lance's little pod both being noticed and attacked?" asked Joe.

"My guess is, we just had bad timing. Some of those pirates were probably in the area," answered Marty.

"If you say so," replied Joe. He was far from convinced, especially since he was the one doing the space walking.

"I'm not saying this is going to be a cakewalk," continued Martin. "However, we can't just do nothing, and by the time the Solar Patrol could get here, they might be long gone. We've got to try something."

"Do you want to tell George what's going on, just in case?" Joe asked.

"That's probably a good idea," answered Martin. "I need to do it now, though, because once we get much closer, our radio communications will be detectable. I'll go do the call."

Joe and Yvette, sat at the control desk while Martin went to the telecommute. "Things could get ugly, you know," said Joe.

"Yeah," laughed Yvette. "When I get a hold of the bastards that stole my ship, you can bet it will be verrrry ugly!"

"Oh, how I'd hate to tangle with you, comrade!" laughed Joe.

"I should think it would be fun," Yvette threw back. They paused for a moment when Martin's voice became audibly louder.

"Dammit, George! I don't have a choice. I can't do this run again. Nicole will have my head. I have to go after what's mine!"

"You can make money on Earth, Marty! Don't risk your life and the lives of those two young people. Our cowboys' days are over, friend!" replied George.

"I'm sorry, George, I have to do this. I just want you to tell Nicole that I love her and if anything happens to me, let her know I was just thinking of my family."

"If you were really thinking of them, you'd never try this crazy thing!" said George.

"Please, just alert the Patrol and keep your fingers crossed for us all," Martin replied.

"I already have, Marty," replied George.

"Oh, and by the way, Gila had mentioned a Dr. Molina who was involved in the research on micro-biosystems. Can you look into his credentials for me and find out what you can?" asked Martin.

"Yeah, sure," said George. "Anything else? I'll do my homework and get back to you. Please be careful, Marty."

"I will George, and thanks, I owe you one."

"You don't owe me a thing. I'm too glad to help a friend. Only wish I could be there with you," replied George.

Martin was about to shut down the telecommute when he received a message. "Hey, what's going on? This is PoPo. I was on my way to pick up a young boy but looks like I'm going to be diverted. Heard all the telecommutes as I was passing by, can you guys use a hand? Over," came the communication from another ship.

"We sure can, PoPo. Could you ferry some spacewalkers over to this big ship for us?" replied Martin as his plan of attack suddenly seemed more plausible.

"Sure. How many people are we talking about?" asked POPO, curious as to what they were going to do.

Martin quickly explained the situation they were in and how they had to get over to that nefarious ship. "I'm so glad you are here. We can really use some help with this. I'm in constant contact with SOHOIII but we are going to have to maintain radio silence very soon." Martin explained as he shut down the telecommute and turned toward Joe and Yvette. "We're going to shut off the automatic systems and fly by manual controls. We can't risk any type of sensor going off on our approach. I'll take the first shift if you two want to get some sleep. Instead of going into stasis, since there's more of us on board to help fight boredom, let's just do eight hours each of flight. How does that sound?"

"I can do it," answered Joe.

"As can I," replied Yvette.

"Good. Then it's settled. Each of us will brief the next pilot at the start of their shift. Joe, you want to go next?" asked Martin.

"No problem. Wake me in eight," Martin's shift was uneventful, which gave him extra time to study the layout of the large ship or small space station. He almost dozed off himself for a moment when the whir of the galactic fax brought him to reality. He picked up the scrolling message and began to read the report George had sent him, about Venus and Dr. Molina.

* * * * *

"Several years ago, a group of scientists sought funding to colonize Venus. They felt it had great potential to support the ever-growing populations of the other planets, as well as provide a place for a long-term prison, so they drew up a proposal. The inter-galactic government gave the go-ahead for the money, with several provisions. One of those provisions was that the work had to come in under budget and within the allotted time frame. It had done neither. The government pulled its funding, and the researchers were left with only an infrastructure of what could have been the most impressive of all space stations.

This action made them very bitter. They vowed to band together, to get investors and create the outpost privately. However, no one was interested. At that point, most of the scientists pulled out, content to return to their jobs at various universities and research centers. Two of them, however, chose to remain. They knew their only hope of continuing their various research projects was through their own means. No help was available at this point.

Serge Molina was a Russian biochemist. He had grown up in a repressed economic region and he resented the Americans, believing they were meddling in his country's affairs. His father had been an official in the Russian government. When capitalism broke out, his father was forced out of office and his family was evicted from their stately home. Serge was accepted to the University because of his brilliance. There was no test score that decade in the entire Soviet Republic, which was higher than his score.

During his six years of study, he conducted a multitude of experiments on animals, plants and some claim he even used human subjects. He had little tolerance for anyone else; the rest of the human race was a mere nuisance. His left eye was white, the result of a chemical burn during his sophomore year in school. It gave his rather large head an even more ghastly appearance, but he couldn't have cared less. He had no intention of sharing his life with anyone else. Women were irritating, with their constant nagging and bitching about every little thing. He had grown up with four older sisters and a domineering mother. He had no use for the female gender. Not that he was gay. He didn't like men, either. Most males he encountered had barely evolved from their primitive ancestors. Power and strength were all that was important. He often wondered why he couldn't simply be left alone with his chemicals and vials and Bunsen burners.

Then he met Doug Konner. Doctor Douglas Konner to be exact. Douglas had been an Olympic swimmer with several gold medals to his name. He had represented the United States in the 2080 Olympics. He got to direct the 2090 World's Fair, which was held on Mars. He came from an upstanding family who resided in the suburbs of Boston. His father was a surgeon, his mother a diplomat. His sister married well but his brother died in a freak accident while the two boys were away at school. From the time Doug was about a year old, women couldn't keep their hands off of him. He was touched, petted, held and hugged, and he loved every moment of it. Doug had the body of an athlete and the tan of a beach bum. His white teeth almost blinded anyone looking at him in direct sunlight. That dazzling smile was a sharp contrast to the dark, brooding features that defined his face. Had he nothing else, Douglas could have been a model. But God had blessed him with an amazing mind, as well. He went to college on full scholarship. Not that he needed it. Eight years later, he emerged with a medical degree, a chemistry degree and a specialization in languages. Something he had taken for fun.

Unlike Serge, Doug loved women. He loved them in any shape or size, color or species. He couldn't get enough. With his Olympic record, his amazing, good looks and promising future, he should have been "The Galaxy's Most Eligible Bachelor", or at least America's sweetheart. However, the daughter of a prominent politician, and news of a child born out of wedlock just after he had completed college dimmed his bright star. He had joined the scientists on Venus, some ten years ago, to find sanctuary from all the bad publicity."

"Martin..." George had added, "This is very alarming. Neither of these men have been seen or heard from in over two years. Not since the project was halted. It's going to be my guess that they could be behind the strange activities on Venus. I'm also sending you the blueprints from the Venus Project. NASA was kind enough to let me hack into their computer and "borrow" the information. But let's not mention that to them, okay?"

"Thanks, again. I see we are up against some formidable thieves," replied Martin.

"Are you ready for me?" asked Joe. He was yawning but dressed and ready for work.

"Oh, sure am," came the reply. "You've got to take a look at this stuff that our good friend George sent us. This is the report he put together about the building of the Venus station and report on a couple possible suspects in this whole thing. He also sent us the blueprints of the facility on Venus. Can you scan them into the computer in case we need to access them later?"

"No problem," answered Joe. "Get some sleep."

"Oh, by the way," continued Martin, "I'm following the vapor trail of our little pirate friend. He's taking us right to that ship behind Venus, just like we thought."

"I got it. See you in sixteen!" said Joe. The young pilot sat down at the controls and logged in his information. He looked over the blueprints that George had sent. He kept the vapor trail in sight. It was a great way to follow the craft at a large distance and Joe had no trouble sighting in on it. "It sure would be great if we could use our scanners over the ship to see in better detail where Yvette's ship and the collectors were, for sure," thought Joe. He knew, however, that this was impossible. The use of any of those types of devices would draw attention to them. They had to avoid this at all costs. He continued his uneventful shift and then woke Yvette as he started to get sleepy.

"Sixteen hours already?" she groaned.

"Wake up lazy!" he said. "It's my turn to crash."

"Poor choice of words but go ahead," she replied.

"Let me give you a run down on the past few hours," said Joe. He proceeded to tell her what had happened during the last two shifts, and about the information that came in from George. He informed her of the vapor trail and to keep her eyes open, and that the traffic was heavy at times. With that, he went to sleep.

Yvette also had little to interfere with smooth flying while she piloted. She noticed the increase in traffic as they passed satellite stations for refueling and repairs, but certainly nothing out of the ordinary. Day by day, the three pilots took turns at the controls. Watching the tireless trail of vapor from the pirate ship. The time finally approached where they all needed to remain awake; Venus was clearly in sight, and so was the ship/station.

As the ship neared the station, the three were startled by a blip-blip coming from Yvette's clothing. "Oh, shit!" she said. "My homing device is going off. I never shut it down!" Quickly, she grabbed it off of her lapel and powered down the small device. The pilots all took a moment to catch their breath and then assessed the situation.

"Do you think they picked anything up?" asked Joe.

"I doubt it. We didn't send the signal and I'm sure that their equipment won't pick up broadcasts from random waves all the time," answered Martin.

"I am so sorry," apologized Yvette. "However, that means my ship is definitely out there and they haven't found the homing device. The ship's power source must still be operational!"

"That's what I was thinking. It's probably still intact. You may have gotten lucky," said Martin.

"The computer indicates that signal came from the exact location Gila mentioned. We might be able to pull this off after all," said Joe.

"Our first piece of real proof," mused Martin. "Once we get near the large ship, Yvette, you'll need to remotely prepare your ship for launch as discreetly and quickly as you know how. Keep in mind that many of the wires have probably been cut by the micro-biosystems, so you'll have some splicing to do once you board. But be fast. Joe and I will begin the retrieval of collectors. We have five missing and you have how many, Yvette?"

"Six, but if you can't get them, that's okay. I'll be happy just to get my ship back."

"We'll need to carry communicators, but they must only be used in an extreme emergency. If we get caught, you haul ass out of here and notify the authorities, okay?" instructed Martin.

"Hopefully, the Texas Star, Kitty Hawk, and the White Nova will be leaving simultaneously," replied Yvette.

"Shall we prepare for a "close encounter"?" joked Martin.

"Yee-ha! Let's go, cowboys! Let's get suited up for a stroll in the park!" hollered Joe.

"PoPo? You ready to pilot two spacewalkers over to the big ship?" asked Martin, who reluctantly broke radio silence.

"I'm right with you and I'll keep them shaded," answered PoPo. "Oh, my God! There she is! How can I ever thank you?" cried Yvette.

"We're not home yet," said Martin. "I have a feeling the fun is just about to begin."

The two marauders quickly disembarked from the Texas Star and quickly latched on to PoPo's pod. They didn't know what to expect once they reached the mammoth ship much less if this craziness was going to work.

"Good luck," whispered Joe to Yvette as they launched toward PoPo.

The two headed towards the White Nova, who was soon in front of them. "God! We'd better find the collectors aboard this mammoth of a ship," thought Martin. He unlatched himself and made his way to the mooring of Yvette's ship while Yvette quickly found her way to the airlock of the White Nova.

"Almost there." signaled Joe, as he could see the mechanisms for the release.

"Now, Martin said for you to take-off as soon as you can get free." He reminded Yvette.

"Not until I know you are back safe. This is a Russian ship. You need to realize I have powerful guns on board." She replied as she started up her controls, but Joe was already making his way to the airlock on the main ship.

"He is on board!" Yvette communicated to Martin, who was also busy suiting up and preparing to intercept collectors and bring them in.

Martin was right. The collectors were stored just ahead of Joe as he hurried to open the cargo bay and release them out into space. Joe was busy activating the homing devices on those that still had them in working order. The rest would have to be hunted down by Martin. Joe worked as quickly as he could and planned on leaving the bay with the last one. PoPo was then to shuttle Joe over to the Kitty Hawk so he could board and bring her back as well. So far so good but he did not realize that Yvette had engaged the enemy.

"Ok, Vic, is it? I'm sitting here with a laser cannon pointed right at your stash of hydrogen. Now if you want your station to explode, you just try and stop our guy from getting the Kitty Hawk, which is our ship to begin with. We could pick Joe up after we vaporize you, or can we get our stuff and exit without a problem." She explained while watching Vic's reaction on the telecommute.

"Well, now I guess we have a slight impasse," Vic replied. 'I thought Reg disconnected all the weapons on board."

"He had, but I did some quick rewiring. And some re-programming, so if you want to take a chance, give me a try. It is my ship again and I have control," laughed Yvette. "Now, if you don't mind, I need to retrieve some collectors and I'll be off."

"If that is what you believe, I'll not stand in your way. Good luck. The boss said just to let you guys go," came Vic's reply with a snarl that scared Yvette.

* * * * *

"I'm stuck in orbit, since the controls are responding so slowly," she shouted.

"Have you tried to manually override your system?" asked Martin.

"Yes, I've tried everything. I think those things are still on board!" Yvette answered back. "I'm losing control!"

"Stay calm, as best you can. Let me send a message to Gila and see if he knows how to kill those suckers! We have some time before things get desperate. We could tow you behind the Texas Star if we have to!" Martin said.

Martin raced to the telecommute to call Gila. No need to maintain radio silence at this point. It was the middle of the night and Lance answered the machine. "What's wrong, Dad?" he asked.

"We found Yvette's ship, and she's in it but she is losing control. We think there're more micro-biosystems on board. I need you to ask Gila what to do about them, if anything."

"Dad, I can help. I've read all of Dr. Molina's research on them and I think I know how to get rid of them. Does she have a Cobalt-60 source on her shuttle?"

"Let me check," Martin said. A minute later he was back. "That's affirmative! Now what?"

"Okay, now she'll need to expose them to a blast of gamma rays; About 250 rems worth, for about twenty minutes, allowing for the thickness of the metal around the console." Lance continued.

"Are you getting this, Yvette?" Martin asked. He had left the channels open so she could hear the conversation.

"Yeah. I'm on it. Is this going to kill them?" she asked.

"It should, and if not, it'll make them sick enough to slow them down. Then you can regain control of your ship," replied Lance. "Where is your cobalt-60 source?"

"There is some in the backup energy pack," replied Yvette.

"You will have to pull it out of its lead casing and set it above the area you wish to irradiate. Then you get out of there and go into a radiation protected airlock till the time is up," explained Lance. "No guarantees here, but it is worth a try."

"Okay, I've got it going. I'll need to reboot the entire system which will take me offline for a few minutes. Talk to you then," Yvette signed off and went to work on her ship.

"Thanks, Lance! If that works, we will all be in your debt. Very impressive, son!" said Martin.

"Let me know if I can help anymore, Dad. Goodnight."

* * * * *

"Martin, we've got trouble. Two ships are appearing on the radar and they're coming directly toward us. I'm going to do the laser, I don't think this is a diplomatic mission," said PoPo, who had been waiting for a fight.

"TEXAS STAR... We recommend you surrender your ship. We have dispatched two of our ships to escort you back to the surface. It is our desire that no one is harmed during this encounter, but we will use force if necessary," boomed an accented voice over the radio.

"Ah, Dr. Molina, I presume?" replied Martin.

"I'm surprised you know my name. You've done your research," he answered from the control center.

"You've set up an amazing operation, but it's no longer of any value since I've put it together and found you. How is your partner, Dr. Konner?" Martin asked.

"I'm impressed. How did you ever link the two of us?"

"Actually, I didn't. There's been an investigation into your disappearances and it's just too coincidental that you both vanished at about the same time," replied Martin.

"I'm sure we could reach an amicable agreement if you care to hear it?" boomed the Russian's voice.

"I sincerely doubt it," answered Martin.

"We are all intelligent human beings. You could be a major benefactor once the price of Hydrogen is forced to increase," said Molina.

"You're trying to halt the flow of Hydrogen!" shouted Martin, suddenly realizing what this crazy man's plan was.

"You catch on quickly, friend. Once the prices increase and we cash in on that situation, we will have the funding to finish this outpost and build our research laboratories."

"You're nuts if you think you can get away with this," said Martin.

"Oh, we will. But just think of what my micro-biosystems could do to fight disease in man. They could be used to devour cancers, open clogged arteries, repair damaged nerves and who knows what else. I just need the funding to bring these ideas to the world."

"The National Science Foundation would, I'm certain, jump at the opportunity to fund your research," encouraged Martin, hoping to stall long enough for Yvette and Joe to escape.

"They would, except for one thing. I have some enemies on the board who will do everything in their power to keep me from my work. They have accused me of atrocities. Idiots, all of them," Martin continued to let him ramble on.

"Yes, but no one individual can stand in the way of true science," added Marty fueling the debate.

"They can sure try..." continued Dr. Molina explaining the details of his present fight with the foundation.

Soon, the Texas Star had pulled in close enough to pick Molina up on the communication screen. Martin almost jumped at the man's appearance. He had not aged well in space. The whitened eye seemed bigger than the other and his face was covered with liver spots. He had to keep the man talking, however. "So, where's your friend, Dr. Konnor, or did you eat him?" asked Martin.

"He's coming now. Would you like to speak with him?"

"Certainly," replied Martin. Soon, the face of a handsome 50-something man filled the screen. Martin was taken with his appearance as well. Not because it was ugly, quite the opposite. He was staring into Joe's face, only twenty years older. "My God," thought Martin.

"Hello Martin," said Dr. Doug Konnor. "Pity we had to meet this way."

"You could simply let us go and we'd be out of your hair in no time," said Martin.

"But you are taking with you enough Hydrogen to pay for the completion of our station," said Dr. Konnor. Martin knew that these were not violent men. They were simply obsessed and misguided by their own desires.

"Dr. Konnor, I'd like you to meet someone. Joe, get on the communicator," responded Martin. The instant the two men saw each other they knew. Like that of twins who are separated and then reunited many years later, there was no doubt that they were related.

"How old are you?" asked Dr. Konnor quietly.

"Twenty-three," answered Joe from the console of the Kitty Hawk. "Do you have any kids?" Joe wasn't too sure why he asked that question. But the resemblance confused him, and he seemed to just blurt it out.

"Only one. A boy whom I have never seen. His name is Joseph Burwich after his mother's family," answered Dr. Konnor.

"What does his mother look like?" asked Joe.

"She's dead, now, but she was the color of the sun with eyes like the sky." The two men stared at each other for a long time. Dr. Molina was obviously confused, however. Martin felt such sorrow for Joe realizing that he had finally found his biological father. "Who is your father, boy?" continued Dr. Konnor.

"Never met the man," answered Joe, about ready to be sick.

"Well, Dr.," began Joe, "I hope you find your son."

"I doubt that, and I wish you could find your father someday," Dr. Konner answered.

"We need to continue this discussion at my facility," said Molina, bringing the conversation back to the matter at hand. "If you will be so kind, Mr. Mercer, as to follow the escort to the surface, we can work out details of an arrangement."

"You're not going to work out any kind of deal with him, are you Martin?" Joe whispered angrily.

"Of course not, stupid, I just had to give Yvette time to fix her ship and get the hell out of here." The ship rocked as a powerful laser blast struck its side.

"That's it, I'm firing back," yelled Joe. "I've engaged the pirate ship. Nailed him!"

"Keep firing," said Martin. "We haven't sustained any real damage yet, but I don't know how long we can hold off two ships." Again, the Texas Star was hit, this time sustaining enough damage to force the sealing off of one section that maintained atmospheric control. "This isn't looking good." Martin said as he was hit again.

"You can't take too many more blasts!" yelled Joe. Without firing a shot, Joe looked up in time to see the attacking ship explode into millions of tiny fireflies.

"I got you, you bastard!" shouted Yvette into the radio. "I told you not to fuck with my ship or my friends!"

"Remind me to never piss you off!" shouted Joe.

"Let's get this other guy," she answered back. It took only a few rounds delivered from PoPo's vessel and the White Nova before that ship, too, was reduced to ashes.

"Russian ships come prepared," bragged Yvette.

"I like that," chimed in Joe who thought he came prepared for a simple Hydrogen run. At this moment, however, he would have given up a few tanks for a good laser cannon.

"Thanks again PoPo. You have been a life saver. Now everyone get out of here," replied Martin.

"Tell the good doctors we'll be seeing them on the news," said Yvette. The four ships sped off in opposite directions. Yvette and the Kitty Hawk back to Earth and the Texas Star and PoPo back to the Lunar Station.

Martin telecommuted with SOHOIII to let them know what had just transpired when Lance grabbed the communication device. "Dad, don't use your stasis chambers. It is possible the micro-biosystems have rewired the chambers to kill whoever activates them!" he yelled. "Just don't use them. Please," he continued.

"What brought this on?" asked Martin.

"I was looking over those notes I found, and they were looking at ways to interfere with those chambers. It started with them trying to make them more efficient and then they discovered ways to make them deadly as well. Just, please don't use them," continued a concerned Lance.

"Son, if you tell me not to use them. You can bet I won't. I trust your expertise in this area. I have to let the others know as well. Love ya, son. I'm on my way back to the lunar station," continued Marty. "I'll have to hurry before they set up their chambers. Joe and Yvette are heading back to Earth."

CHAPTER 10

EARTH

"I'll go stabilize all the collectors I hauled aboard and check for damage." Mumbled Martin to himself as he made a mental checklist of everything that needed to get done. At this moment he really missed Joe, as he could use a helping hand. He felt exhausted but invigorated from this adventure, however he could not wait to get back to the comfort of earth. Martin reflected on the changes he knew he would have to make back home. But first he decided to call Nicole.

"Hello dear," Nicole answered. She had just come in from the store and was setting down her purchases.

"All safe and sound...I'm coming home. On my way back to the Lunar Station for now," said Martin.

"Well, dinner won't wait that long," she joked. "How was the expedition?" She sensed tenseness in his voice. "You look tired. Are you sure you are, ok?"

"Oh, just routine, you know..."

"Yeah, I'm sure. I'll hear the truth when you get here. I love you!"

"Back at you, honey. Bye." Martin closed the telecommute just as a new message came in from Popo.

"Bad news, Marty."

"Why? What's up?" Martin asked.

"You took a couple of those hits pretty hard. You've got some damage mostly on the starboard side...nothing you can't limp to the

Lunar Space Station with. But you will need some repair work before re-entry. I'm going to stick with you all the way back just in case we get visited again. They know you have all those collectors on board." Answered back PoPo trying to assess Martin situation.

"We don't have to worry about Dr. Molina anymore," Martin replied.

"What makes you so certain? And besides, if your ship is damaged, that makes it easier to board should anyone else decide to relieve you of your ore. You need me to follow you back in case you run into trouble again," replied PoPo.

"Thanks for your advice PoPo. I'm so tired right now I'm having a hard time grasping the situation I'm in."

"That may be, but as it stands right now, you'll never survive re-entry to the earth's atmosphere," replied PoPo.

"Fine, then I'll repair the ship before I leave the Lunar Station. I'll have to keep someone on board at all times and I guess I'll need your help with the repairs if you wouldn't mind. I'll pay you of course?" replied Martin.

"Yeah, I can help since we messed up watching Lance. I can radio ahead to Apollowalla and see if she can line up some more services." PoPo replied.

"Don't you wonder who it was that planted those micro-biosystems?" asked Martin. "I mean, the scientists had to have an associate either on earth or on the Lunar Station. They couldn't have done it themselves."

"Yeah, I sure do, but our chances of finding the bastards are slim."

"Whoever it is, if they're on the Lunar Station, we've got to be really careful. They could sabotage us to burn up on re-entry; something I'm certain Dr. Molina would love to see right now." Martin sat in silence as he began to think that their plan was to re-take the ships after everyone died while in their stasis sleep. Maybe that is why they got away so easily. Shaking his head, he got up and headed to the cargo hold where he needed to remove all the lead shielding on the collectors' electronics before irradiating the chamber for several hours with the cobalt 60 source.

* * * * *

Martin's thoughts turned to Joe as he finished up with the Cargo hold and really began to miss his helping hand. He had been careful not to say anything too derogatory about Dr. Konnor. He knew the story of the promising young surgeon, whose out-of-wedlock son with a prominent politician's daughter made the prospects for his career a little more difficult and her life with her father was near intolerable, only because of all the negative publicity. The story was really a tragedy; three lives damaged by one night of passion. He could not imagine what Joe was going through right now, but Martin wanted to help him in any way he could.

Martin decided to give Apollowalla a call on her special frequency to see if she had any news on the upheaval in the Hydrogen industry, and to let her know more about his situation. The biosystem listened in awe as Martin related the details of his adventure.

"I've gotten reports of at least fifteen other runners who have had their collectors stolen in the past month," she volunteered.

"Good Lord! They could have built "Space Palace" with that kind of cash!" Martin asked her about Yvette and Joe to see if she has gotten any updates on their location. "Apollowalla, could you prepare a list of all the thefts that have occurred and cross-reference them with the time they were on the Lunar Station as well as their liftoff times from earth? By the way, is that a new voice synthesizer I detect?" Martin asked.

"Why, yes, it is. Do you like it?" she asked.

"No comparison to the old one, far better. Nice going," complimented Marty.

"Thank-you Martin. I'll do my best on getting a list and well, I'm sure that we can help you with your repairs, but I can't let you dock here at the Lunar Station, in case you are still contaminated with those nasty micro-biosystems," replied Apollowalla sternly.

"What!?" replied Martin.

"You can refuel in space and PoPo can spray the ship down with the new synthetic lubricant to prevent the ship from overheating on re-entry. The lubricant really cuts down on the friction the ships encounter on re-entry, but you have to fly around the earth a few more times to slow down otherwise you come in too fast. The friction may heat up the ship, but it acts to slow down your re-entry speed, so to compensate for that you have to take a little longer to get down. A small trade-off for preventing the heat up of the ship, especially with all those hydrogen collectors on board. Maybe next time you do another run the elevator will be finished. Can you imagine how busy I will be monitoring all the deliveries in the elevator as well as all the dockings? I get panic attacks thinking about it. Well, I'll get working on all these projects in front of me. Over, Apollowalla out".

Marty began a badly needed rest. His sleep was deep; exhausted from the past few days, while his mind buzzed with questions. He longed to sit down and talk to Dr. Konnor, to find out what happened. Why he hadn't stayed around and fought for his son?

Martin awoke to the soft hum of the telefax. As promised, Apollowalla was sending the information he had requested. He settled into the task of trying to find a common link between all the ships that had experienced some type of theft. In a matter of seconds, it was obvious; too obvious. All the ships involved had stopped at the Lunar Station for re-fueling. Martin kept digging. All the collectors were made by the same Japanese manufacturer. NASA knew of every ship's scheduled flight plan and all but six of them left from Houston Space Center. Finally, they were all on the Lunar Space Station at the same time as Vic and Reg. There was also a telefax addressed to Joe from Dr. Konner.

"Wow," thought Martin, "This is the strangest run I've ever done and who knows what will happen next." Martin could still see PoPo's ship near-by. PoPo kept his word about following alongside as the two ships approached the area around the Lunar Station.

"PoPo, are you up? Just want to say thank-you for staying with me," telecommuted Martin. How are things looking out there?

"We've got some pretty weak spots, but we should be able to make the necessary repairs. I was just figuring out which ones to do first once we get to the station area. Apollowalla informed me that we would not be able to dock the Texas Star at the station, but we will have to wing it in space. That won't make the repairs impossible just a little slower and a little more complicated. Anyhow I've been working on the problem," replied PoPo.

"That's good enough for me." Replied Martin as he guided the ship into a stable position. Just then Lance came over the telecommute.

"Hi Dad!"

"How's it going, Dr. Lance?" Martin asked proudly as he still could not believe his son had an intern position on SOHO III.

"Martin, I'm so glad you're doing better and back at the Lunar Station," Gila chimed in, while Lance was almost in tears. They had been extremely concerned as they had both watched the excitement, unable to do anything but worry.

"I'm just fine, Gila, a little tired, but good. The ship has sustained some damage, but PoPo has agreed to help with the repairs. I should be back home in a couple days now," replied Martin.

"Can I show you what we have done in the plant laboratory? I've got a surprise planned." Though he was in a hurry to get the ship fixed, he decided to indulge the accommodating biosystem and his son. He marveled at the new growth, just since they had left the station. Orchids, the size of human heads, provided an archway to the lab. He had been successful in his elusive strawberry-banana tree tests. Laid out on a table was a succulent picnic of the juiciest hybrid fruits, and steamed vegetables that Gila has created. Well at least SOHOIII has an abundant food supply. Martin all of a sudden felt very hungry and longed for the pleasure of eating real unprocessed foods! "That is really a beautiful sight, you guys are something else." Moaned Martin jealous of the feast they grew.

Martin stayed up for a bit longer to talk to Gila about the virility of the micro-biosystems and just what could be expected. He had some in-sight for Martin, but told him, quite the systems; he and Lance had been studying them ever since we uncovered them, but Lance had been reading the notes from the pod, and probably knew as much as he did. Martin thanked him and turned in.

That next morning, Martin evaluated what gear he had on the Texas Star that would help PoPo with the ship's repairs, and laughed as he thanked Joe under his breath for insisting that Helen get those spare parts on the ship. There were several spare outside panels and lots of extra insulating foam. All of which Martin would not have on board if it hadn't been for Joe's meticulous care for detail. PoPo extended a tether line to the Lunar Space Station to help stabilize the Texas Star. Martin could see the Entrance Tunnel, which was always a welcomed sight to him, only this time he wasn't going in.

"Texas Star, Arturia is standing by to give you all the assistance you need. She's a female biosystem, but don't you give me one bit of male ego; she's a great mechanic!" Apollowalla's voice seemed to fill the whole ship as it came over the intercom. She's here to give PoPo an extra hand in this repair situation. Sorry Martin, I just can't let you enter the station," continued Apollowalla.

"How long did PoPo estimate for repairs?" asked Martin.

"It should take about three hours, providing everything goes well. It may go even faster, depending on how well this plant-lady works out. And, I'll have you know he plans on using some of those spare parts you told us you had on board.

The three hours includes spraying down the ship with the anti-friction lubricate to lessen the heat up on re-entry," came Apollowalla's response. "I feel really bad about not letting you use one of the repair bays so I'll help you guys through this as best I can," she continued.

"Okay," replied Martin as he realized she was right by not letting him enter the station.

"Did you have a chance to look at the data I sent you earlier about the ships and people that were here at the station?" asked Apollowalla in her new voice simulator.

"Yes, I did some checks and correlations. It didn't take long." Marty answered.

"Marty, let me take a look at what you've got, and we can go from there. I'm just as anxious to find out who's behind all this nonsense as you are, especially if it's someone from my space station."

"Here you go, let's see if you come up with the same conclusions I did." Replied Martin as he sent her his data analysis charts and about that time PoPo showed up outside the Texas Star to start the necessary repairs. "I've got to go, PoPo is outside, and we are going to start putting this ship back together."

* * * * *

After about an hour, Apollowalla came back on. "Well, I agree with your findings, Vic and Reg were here when each of the tampered ships were in dock, but there were never any reports of break-ins while they were here. Someone would have to have gotten on board without being detected. Wouldn't you think that at least one of the pilots would have something? Unless...unless these micro-biosystems had somehow been planted on the pilots themselves and they could have carried them aboard like a virus." Mumbled Apollowalla as she continued to examine the data analysis Martin sent over.

"I hadn't thought of that possibility, but I think these little systems would have to be planted directly in the collectors or at least put on the one-way opening valve." Replied Martin.

"Why? They're microscopic. They could pass through minute cracks in the hardware."

"For any other instrumentation this would be true. However, we're dealing with collectors, which must be totally sealed to prevent the loss of any ore we gather," answered Martin.

"Then, how?" continued Apollowalla.

"I really didn't want to say this before, but;"

"I know," she said. "You think it was someone who works here at the station."

"Look at the facts. It had to be someone who could get in and out very easily, without anyone suspecting them. Someone who does the final pre-flight checks and cargo clearances. This might take more work on your part as you take a closer look at the people who have clearance to get aboard the ships prior to giving them the OK for departure from the station."

"You're right, Marty. This may take a while to solve, in the meantime I'll watch out for Vic and Reg and put out a "RAS" (restrain at sight) for them. I doubt that they will be back, though. I sure would like to interrogate them."

"Sorry, I know this will be hard, but now that we have a heads up and have an idea of what to look for, you might get a break."

"I hope these crooks aren't doing this just for money!" She said adamantly. "Oh, PoPo is calling you. The ship's ready. I can see now that this mess may involve a few more people than I originally thought. Hmmm PoPo." Mumbled Apollowalla as fear began to set in. She realized he had access to all the ships and his presence would not be questioned. A look of panic came across Apollowalla's face.

"Did you just say PoPo?" asked Martin. "He has been crawling all over my ship inside and out, OMG. I think I'm going to be sick." Replied Martin as he fell off his chair. Let me know if you find anything else. I might be able to help from Earth, since I can use the NASA computers and since you helped me with these stupid repairs, but first I'm going to have to decontaminate the ship again. It may be a while before I can remove the tether line."

"Ok. I'll tell everyone you are ill and will head back when you feel better. That should give you some time. I hope you will make it back without any problems," she replied.

"Oh, now, don't go doing self-hydroponics! I'll be in contact with you whether I'm up here or back home. You realize I'm leaving my son on SOHOIII, so I will have to come back and pick him up. Hopefully this situation will be solved by the time I come back. Don't know if I can stand another run like this one has turned out to be."

"Oh, by the way, Joe and Yvette have both landed safely on Earth. That should make things a little better."

"Now clear me for my return trip," he said, giving the big biosystem a thumbs up. Marty ran down to the cargo bay, where PoPo was standing with Arturia.

"Apollowalla was right," PoPo said with a smile. "This girl is gooooooood!"

Martin was about to answer but first he had to shake off his paranoia and said, "Great. Let's get the ship ready for takeoff." He paid Arturia for her services and thanked her again.

"Texas Star has clearance for take-off." Came Apollowalla's new voice. Martin wasn't about to miss the old one. "Whenever you feel up to it Martin, just let me know when you release the tether."

"Unfortunately, I'm too ill to take her back home at the moment. Give me a day or two so I can sleep this infection off," said Martin making sure PoPo heard his reply and would not suspect that Martin was going to have to work fast at decontamination before attempting a return to Earth, a mere 250 miles away.

"Just let me know when you are ready," Apollowalla replied.

Marty thanked PoPo and Arturia again, and as soon as they were off the ship, he locked it down and began the decontamination process. "I have to find the strength to do this." Said Martin to himself as he removed the lead shielding on the first of the collectors and pulled up the SOHOIII station on the com.

"Hi Dad," came Lance who seemed in good spirits.

"Son, I think possibly PoPo might have had something to do with planting the micro-biosystems, so you and Gila have to check out the station. Mind you, it is just a suspicion, but we have to act on it." Advised Martin in a serious and urgent reply.

"Gila has already been doing that very thing. He figured since a ship and several of our collectors were stolen from here there was a chance that we too might run into problems. He has been clearing areas ever since we discovered what it was that brought these issues about," replied Lance.

"Well, I guess I didn't raise such a fool," laughed Martin. "I could really be using your help about now, as I have to clear the ship again all by myself without raising any questions. So, if anyone asks, I'm recovering from a stomach problem and will be taking off soon. Joe and Yvette are already down on Earth, which takes a load of worry off. I believe they are cleaning their ships in quarantined areas. This stunt of whoever is behind this is really getting costly."

"Wish I could be there to help you as well," answered Lance. "Please Dad get home safely. I need to know that you are ok as soon as you land. I love you, Dad."

"I'm so proud of you even though this came about in such an unconventional manner. Love you too son, over." Martin replied.

He quickly got off so Lance would not see the tears in his eyes. He didn't know what brought them on, but he did know he had a wonderful son. Martin continued the process of clearing the cargo hold until he could hardly stand but he could rest while this area was undergoing irradiation. He would rest in-between exposures as he let the Cobalt-60 Gamma ray source exposed the ship one section at a time. He really has to have his wits about him when it comes the time to pilot this ship down, not much room for error and he wasn't at all sure how the lubricant coating placed on the outside would affect the re-entry process.

* * * * *

Martin started feeling better as he got the upper hand on the cleaning chore and felt better rested after a day of naps and a night's rest.

"Apollowalla, can you get me a top security clearance for my landing at Houston Space Center? I know I have the routine clearance, but we need to get me down with priority." Martin asked as he pulled up Apollowalla's com. "Also explain that my landing might be a little unusual."

"You realize that means your wife and daughter can't meet you, don't you?"

"I know. I'll see them soon enough. I think it's really important, though to get this sucker down safely."

"I agree," she said. "I'll do it for you."

"Thanks." Replied Martin.

After about forty-five minutes, Apollowalla came back with an all clear. "That's great news. This trip should be interesting, possibly a little bumpy but I should be alright." said Martin as he prepared to untether the ship from the Lunar Space Station.

"Good flying, if anyone could bring the Texas Star down it is you, Martin," came a re-assuring Apollowalla. "Buckle in and leave the com open. It is sure to be a rough landing, hope PoPo's repairs hold up, and I sure hope those little critters did not damage anything before you nailed them." She laughed.

"The emergency crews should be standing by, I did the best I could but, I wouldn't make any guarantees." grimaced Martin, not at the thought of the landing but at hearing Apollowalla laugh.

"To say bumpy was an understatement. Shit, there goes some of the thermal panels, but I'm holding steady, though. This is my second time around the Earth which is bringing my speed down a little." Martin talked louder and louder hoping Apollowalla was still listening. It was somehow comforting to have her in there with him. The turbulence increased; the ship shook violently. Martin used every bit of strength to bring the ship in.

"Texas Star, we are ready to assist you. Emergency landing procedures are in place," came a faceless voice over the intercom from Houston Space Center. It continued, "you have priority landing. We are aware that you are carrying hazardous cargo."

"Thank you, Houston. I will be touching down within five minutes. Hope I don't need your emergency services!" Martin said. Piloting the ship was now taking all his strength. The shuttle bounced and bumped its way through the atmosphere and down the landing strip; seemingly to turn minutes into hours.

"Down!" shouted Marty. "Every bone in my body is in a different place, but I'm on the ground." The shuttle ran off the runway and skidded nearly two hundred yards before coming to a stop in the scrub surrounding the landing strip. It appears that those micro biosystems did affect some of the landing sensors. Immediately, dozens of rescue techs surrounded the craft, waiting to help Martin in case he had gotten hurt in the landing. He managed to emerge, smiling broadly. "Marty, you must have had one hell of a ride!" said John Mc Douglas, his brother-in-law. "I promised Nicole that since she couldn't be here, I would. Jesus! Looks like you were in a war!"

"You don't know the half of it, John," said Martin as he grudgingly sat down on the stretcher bound for the med station.

"It may be a while before I get my earth legs back," said Martin, "but when I do, John, I'd like to talk to you about that job you mentioned...."

Joe was waiting for Martin across from the runway. He was allowed that far because of his pilot status. He was a most welcomed sight. He was waiting as close as they allowed. When the two finally got near, Martin handed Joe a letter that he had placed in his suit pocket a while back. Martin got the printout off the computer aboard the ship and knew he wanted Joe to have it. Slowly, Joe opened up the folded papers and read the first line. "Dear son, I cannot believe that after all these years...." He stopped reading. He looked at Martin and then the letter. Silently, he folded it back and slid it into the trash bin as he reached for Martin's hand. He looked back at Martin, "I've done fine up to now without his input and now I will do even better," commented Joe.

"Dr. Konnor is more of a fool than a thief," said Martin when he saw Joe throw the letter away.

"What do you mean?' asked Joe.

"Any man that loses the love and respect of a son like you is the biggest fool I know." Replied Martin as he looked through the window in the ambulance shuttle and saw a rising moon. He could just make out the location of the wondrous Lunar Station where life's dramas were unfolding just as here on Earth.

Joe wasn't quite sure what Martin was talking about perhaps he got a bump on the head, but proceeded to tell him he was meeting Yvette and her grandfather in Paris for a dinner at their favorite restaurant.

Martin just smiled and knew he would save the computer file for Joe whenever he was ready to read it.

HYDROGEN RUNNER

Earth has become civilized.
The only fuel used these days is Hydrogen.
Out near the sun where we collect the Hydrogen, with pirates it's a little less civilized. My name is Martin Mercer I'm a Hydrogen Runner. To be a runner you have to think on your feet. Act without thinking. Use your instincts. Because on a run, you are reduced to one basic instinct, to Survive!

ISBN 9781518625671
90000
9781518 625671